FOREIGN AFFAIRS

HUGH FLEETWOOD was born in England in 1944. At the age of 18 he went to live in France; at 21, he moved to Italy, where he remained for the next fourteen years. He had his first exhibition in 1970 at the Festival dei Due Mondi in Spoleto; in 1971 he published his first novel, *A Painter of Flowers*, for which he also designed the jacket, as he did for his second novel, *The Girl Who Passed for Normal*, winner of the John Llewellyn Rhys Memorial Prize. His fifth novel, *The Order of Death*, was made into a film starring Harvey Keitel and John Lydon (Johnny Rotten). His most recent one-man show, at the Calvert Gallery in London, coincided with the reissue of six of his books by Faber & Faber's *Faber Finds* series. In 2012, he was cited in David Malcolm's *The British and Irish Short Story Handbook* as a key figure in the development of the English short story; his newest publication, "How the Story Ends", will appear in the anthology *Speak My Language* in November 2015. Hugh Fleetwood currently lives in London.

I0564324

By Hugh Fleetwood

A Painter of Flowers (1972)
The Girl Who Passed for Normal (1973)
Foreign Affairs (1974)
A Conditional Sentence (1975)
A Picture of Innocence (1976)
The Order of Death (1977)
An Artist and a Magician (1978)
The Beast (1979)
The Godmother (1980)
The Redeemer (1981)
Fictional Lives (1982)
A Young Fair God (1983)
A Dance to the Glory of God (1984)
A Dangerous Place (1985)
Paradise (1986)
The Past (1987)
Man Who Went Down With His Ship (1988)
The Witch (1989)
The Mercy Killer (1991)
Brothers (1999)
L & I (2004)
The Dark Paintings (2006)
The Other Half (2008)

FOREIGN AFFAIRS

HUGH FLEETWOOD

VALANCOURT BOOKS

Foreign Affairs by Hugh Fleetwood
First published by Hamish Hamilton in 1973
First American edition published by Stein and Day in 1974
First Valancourt Books edition 2015

Published by Valancourt Books, Richmond, Virginia
http://www.valancourtbooks.com

ISBN 978-1-943910-09-0 (trade paperback)
Also available as an electronic book.

All Valancourt Books publications are printed on acid free paper that
meets all ANSI standards for archival quality paper.

Set in Dante MT

PREFACE

Re-reading *Foreign Affairs* some forty-three years after I wrote it, I was struck by two things. The first was that while later I might have done things differently, I wasn't at all ashamed of my youthful effort, and felt that, nasty as it was, the story still worked. The second was that the underlying theme that I have come to see runs through virtually all my work was here almost nakedly on show.

Again and again, however different my individual plots and settings, and however often I have set off intending to do something quite else, I have found myself writing about an "artist" —whether a writer, a painter, or in the case of *Foreign Affairs* a musician—who either commits a murder, or gains a knowledge of murder and ends up condoning it. And ironically, as a result finds his or her art, or even humanity, enriched.

Being so struck, I then went on to reflect that while for a novel to be counted a success the story must, as I say, "work", for a novel to be of more than passing interest there must also be what some might call a sub-text and Henry James termed a "Figure in the Carpet", but I prefer to think of as a body that the author keeps more or less hidden beneath the surface of his or her tale. A body that nevertheless constantly threatens to—and sometimes does—bob up into the light, and of which the reader is always vaguely aware. To be horrified by, disquieted by, amused by, but always, with luck, intrigued by. A body, moreover, that however much the author pretends otherwise, and however hard he or she has tried to remove all trace of him or herself from the surface, tends on closer inspection to bear a close resemblance to that author—if not to reveal his or her true face.

Hugh Fleetwood
London, 2015

I

Paolo Levin opened his eyes. He looked at the red plastic clock on the table by his bed. Eleven. He looked up at the photographs on the wall. Giant framed photographs. Of himself. Paolo in the city. Paolo in the country. Paolo in blue jeans. Paolo in a heavy sweater. Paolo in bathing shorts. Paolo nude.

Then he looked at the posters on the wall. He read his name. Paolo Levin. A concert … pianist, Paolo Levin. A concert … soloist, Paolo Levin. A recital. Paolo Levin. Paolo in Florence. Paolo in Siena. Paolo in Catania, in Munich, Berlin, and Paris. . . .

He felt reassured. He closed his eyes.

Elaine would call soon. They would talk for half an hour or so. Then he would get up and make some coffee and take a shower. After that he would go out and buy a newspaper, and something to eat for lunch. When he had read the paper, and had his lunch, and spoken to a few other friends on the phone he would … he should practice, he supposed. But unless the weather was bad, or Elaine was busy, or he really had nothing else to do, he knew that he wouldn't. He would go to the beach, or go out with his camera and take some photographs and hope he met someone he knew who could take some photographs of *him*. Or he would go and buy a book and sit outside somewhere and read.

He opened his eyes again and looked at the closed shutters and wondered what the weather was like. He hoped it was fine.

The red telephone on the table by his bed rang. He lifted the receiver and said, "Hello, how are you? Recovered?"

"Paul?" a hesitant voice said.

"Oh, it's you." He frowned. He didn't feel like speaking to his mother—especially as she was going to complain.

"You could sound a little more friendly."

"I just woke up."

"It's eleven o'clock."

"I was out late last night."

"Paul," his mother repeated. He imagined he heard her sigh.

7

"Yes?"

"Why didn't you tell us you were playing in Milan last Monday? I would have liked to come. So would your father."

"You know I don't like family or friends listening to me."

"Well, I think you might have told us anyway. And you could have come up to see us since you were so near. We haven't seen you for six months."

"I had to get back to Rome immediately to see someone. How did you find out?"

"I saw a little review in the *Corriere*."

"Oh. That."

"Yes, dear. It wasn't very good."

"I thought it was. 'Great sensibility and musicality.'"

"'Marred by careless execution.'"

"It didn't say that."

"Well, something very like."

Paolo sighed.

His mother continued. "Paul, dear, do you practice enough? Do you practice every day? I know that *all* the great pianists do. And if you can do something well it seems so silly to me to ruin it just out of laziness."

"I can't help it if I'm lazy."

"Of course you can, dear."

"Anyway, I do practice."

"I was calling you yesterday all day and you were never in, and I called you the day before yesterday."

"I don't answer the phone when I'm practicing."

"Were you practicing yesterday?"

"No. I went to the beach."

"Oh," his mother said in quiet triumph.

"Anyway, after I've given a concert I always give myself a week off."

"You treat yourself very well. But if you give yourself a week off I do think you could have come up to see us. Even if it was just for lunch. I know you had to see someone, but even so—"

"I'll be up at Christmas."

"Yes, dear."

"And you know I really do practice. It's just that I prefer to wait until I can see a concert's about a month away, and then I do nothing else—eight, nine hours a day." He bit his lips. He felt furious with himself. His mother spoke so calmly, so patiently, with such an air of defeat—and yet she always managed to make him feel weak and defensive, and tell lies.

She said now, more calmly and patiently than ever, "Oh, well, I suppose you know best, dear, but it doesn't seem the ideal way of going about things, and it does seem a shame, and—"

"How are you all?"

"We're very well. Your father's out at the moment. Aunt Mary's here."

"Oh, my God. And you wanted me to come and see you with her there! Are you mad?"

"Well, she is a bit difficult."

"I guess Dad's taking her for a trip round the lake on the steamer?"

"Yes, he is, actually."

"That's all he ever does when she's there."

"Well, she is his sister. We have to get her out of the house somehow and she does like the lake." His mother laughed. "Oh, and I got a letter from your grandmother."

"Isn't she ever going to die?"

"She said she's feeling very healthy. She thinks she's getting tired of Florida. Everyone's so old there, she said. She wants to move somewhere else."

"Ah."

"She said when are you going to get married, because she would like to make some of her money over to you while she's still alive but she wants an excuse for doing it. So she said if you get married she will."

"Hell," Paolo said. "Blackmailing old bitch. If I thought I was never going to get her money I guess I just might do it, but since I am going to anyway, and she can't live much longer, I'm damned if I'll give her the satisfaction of seeing me rich and miserable. If you write, tell her I'm thinking about it, but if she wants an excuse, what's wrong with my birthday?"

"She doesn't like to think about birthdays."

"How old is she now, for God's sake?"

"She must be ninety-three."

"How disgusting."

"Oh, Paul—" and his mother went on to speak about all her other relatives, and about what she had been doing that summer, and what she was going to do that winter.

It was eleven-thirty when Paolo finally said goodbye and hung up. He lay back in his bed and felt exhausted. The day had started badly.

Five minutes later the phone rang again. This time Paolo lifted the receiver more carefully, prepared for whoever might be on the line.

"*Who* have you been talking to?"

A nasal Bostonian voice. Elaine. He smiled. "Thank God it's you. My mother has been on the phone for half an hour."

"You poor dear. Where is she?"

"Oh, safely up in Stresa. But—you know. Why didn't I go up to see them when I was in Milan on Monday. Why don't I practice more."

Elaine laughed.

"I guess I should just be thankful that she only calls once every three months."

"It's your own fault in any case. You should never have persuaded them to come over."

"How could I know they'd want to *live* here. I only said they should come and visit me because I didn't want to drag back to the States that year. I never dreamed they'd stay."

"They never think of going back to America?"

"No. Not for a moment. It's almost three years now. Still, it could be worse. They could have come to live here in Rome."

Elaine laughed. "They wanted to be near you in their old age."

"Well, I think it was very tactless of them. Why did they think I left America if not to get away from them? And after all, my mother left Italy when she was a year old. There can't be any great attraction to the motherland for her, or anything like that. Anyway, let's talk about something else. What's the weather like?"

"Beautiful."

"Good. Because my mother's made me so nervous I shall be in a bad mood all day, and I'd never be able to practice. Shall we go to the beach?"

At twelve o'clock Paolo got out of bed. He made some coffee, took a shower, put on some blue jeans and a white T-shirt, and went out onto his balcony. It *was* a beautiful day. He went into his living room and looked at the paintings and sketches of himself that various friends had done. Then he sat down in an armchair in the sun and lit his first cigarette of the day.

He looked at his piano and thought of the review his mother had read in the paper. "Great sensibility and musicality—above all in his performance of Schubert's posthumous sonata, spoiled somewhat by a certain technical carelessness." Romantic nonsense. Whoever had written that couldn't have been further from the truth. It was his technical ability alone that had got him to the end of the work with as few mistakes as he had made. That got him to the end of everything he played. If he had relied on sensibility and musicality he wouldn't have been able to play a note, any more than he would have been able to ask for directions in an unknown foreign language in an unknown foreign country. He found his way through the music only by following, with a sense of desperation at times, all that he had learned—as he would have been able to understand the directions in that foreign country only if they were given in sign language. It was when he stopped to consider the unknown world of "musicality and sensibility"—as if trying to utter a word in that foreign language—that his hands refused to do exactly what he had taught them to do, and he hit a wrong note.

He had more than a month before his next concert, he thought with relief. He looked at the calendar above the piano. September 18. Then he closed his eyes and lay back in the sun and realized that he should have known, an hour and a half ago when he had wakened, that today was going to be a bad day. He should have known that when the telephone rang at eleven it would not be Elaine. September 18. March 18. Exactly six months to the day. Six months ago....

He had wakened at eleven and the telephone had rung and

he had picked it up and said, "Hello, how are you?" There had been no reply, and he had thought it had been a wrong number, and had forgotten about it by the time Elaine called him five minutes later. But that afternoon, at five o'clock, when the police had called and had asked him to come, immediately—and he had gone around to Christopher's apartment and been asked to identify the corpse—it was then, standing by the bloody bed, that he realized that that call, at eleven, had been made by Christopher. Christopher, calling to say goodbye; or calling to ask Paolo to come to him. . . .

He put out his cigarette. It would have been out of the question to practice today. Out of the question to do anything today except go to the beach, eat, get drunk, play cards, go to a movie. Christopher, his mother . . . he stood up and his mouth twitched with irritation. Pursuing him, checking up on him, trying to pin him down, trying to trap him, trying to make him feel guilty. . . .

He went into his mirror-lined hall and, taking his camera from the coat rack where it hung, left the apartment. He ran down the stairs and out into the street; a deep, narrow street, and dark after the brightness of his rooms on the top floor.

He went down an alley and came out into Via Cavour; out into the sun. He paused and breathed in. He smelled the heat and the traffic fumes, and the smell was pleasant to him. He smiled up at the blue sky. Since he had decided he was going to have a bad day he would probably enjoy himself—have rather a good day, in fact. He hoped so. But first, the newspaper. There was a stand on the corner, but he didn't like to buy his paper there; he preferred to walk a hundred yards up the road to a little shop. There he could thumb through all the magazines he would never buy.

He went in and smiled at the woman behind the counter, and then turned to the rack on the wall opposite her and started thumbing through the pages of *Newsweek*. Then *A.B.C.* Then *Stop.* There was no news that interested him. The usual economic crises. The usual people pregnant, about to be married, about to be divorced.

As he flicked through the magazines someone came into the shop and stood next to him and started doing the same. After a couple of minutes Paolo glanced up to see a tall, very thin boy with an enormous mop of brown curly hair around his very thin face. But the boy wasn't doing quite the same as him. Yes, he was flicking through the magazines in the same way. But he wasn't looking at them. He was looking at Paolo.

Paolo lowered his eyes and turned back toward the counter. He picked up *La Stampa* and paid for it and went to the door of the shop. Pausing for a moment, he looked back over his shoulder. The tall boy was no longer flicking through the magazines, or even pretending to look at them. He was staring at Paolo, and his eyes in his thin—appallingly thin—face seemed black. His mouth was slightly open, and its lips were very wide and wet.

Paolo felt embarrassed and uncomfortable, and started to walk down the street. There had been something obscene about the boy. Something frightening. He shivered, even though he was in the sun, and felt suddenly tired and afraid. Today wasn't going to be bad. Today was going to be dreadful. Because of course it had been in that same shop that he had seen Christopher for the first time. Had looked up and seen someone staring at him; someone who had said, "Excuse me, are you American?" Someone who, when he met him again by chance in a friend's house two weeks later, had introduced himself as Christopher Rawlings. It was there, at the friend's house, that they had started to talk, become friendly. But the first time he had seen Christopher had been in that newsagent's shop, when Christopher had asked him for directions—he had wanted to find St. Peter's in Chains—and had thought Paolo was American because he had been looking through *Time* magazine. That had been three years ago.

He walked down the street and looked in shop windows and tried not to think about Christopher. Christopher looking at him in the newsagent's; Christopher talking to him; becoming friendly with him; becoming almost a brother to him ... Only Paolo had never wanted a brother. He didn't want any sort of family. He had left his home, left America, when he was fourteen, to get away from his family. He didn't want anyone.

He had had a brother, and his brother had died. And Christopher had died. In his bloody bed, with a hole in his head and, on the floor by the bed, a small black gun. A dead Christopher, naked except for a brown glove on his right hand. On the glove there had been traces of cordite, which had made the police conclude that Christopher had been wearing the glove when he pulled the trigger. A few of the more scandalous newspapers had suggested that someone else could have worn the glove to shoot the gun, and then put the glove on Christopher's hand. But there had been no evidence to support this hypothesis, and a verdict of suicide had been brought in by the coroner.

Paolo glanced at his watch. He had an hour before Elaine picked him up. But he no longer felt like walking around, taking photographs. He would go home and read the paper. As he turned down the alley, out of Via Cavour, he looked over his shoulder once more. There, thirty yards away, staring at him, following him, was the tall thin boy. He stopped when he saw Paolo turn; but not before Paolo had noticed three things about him that he hadn't noticed in the newsagent's. The first was that, in spite of the warmth of the day, the boy was dressed in a long, heavy woolen sweater, thick cord trousers, and a tweed jacket. The second was that when the boy moved these clothes hung off him and flapped around; so that whereas before he had seemed merely thin, he was in fact completely emaciated. The third thing that Paolo noticed was that the boy was crippled. He appeared to hop rather than walk, for one leg—the left—swung back and forth inside its baggy brown trouser leg. The swing had no relation to the movements of the rest of the body; and the foot at the end of it touched the ground only at odd and irregular intervals.

Paolo wondered for a second whether he should go up to the boy and ask him why he was following him and what he wanted. He would have, he told himself, if the boy had been anything other than what he was. But he couldn't go up to a crippled winter-clad skeleton and ask him a rational question and expect a rational answer. No. The boy was obviously mad—and it was best to get away from him. Paolo ran down the alley, along his street, into his door, up the stairs, and into his apartment.

With the door closed behind him he relaxed. He looked at his tanned healthy reflection, then went into the living room and sat down. He was glad to be home.

Suddenly he started to feel angry with himself. Twice in one day he had been made to feel weak and defensive. First with his mother, and now with that mad cripple. Twice in one day was too much. He should have gone up to the cripple and challenged him. Even the mad had their logic. Still . . . now he was at home, and he would spend the afternoon lying on the beach. Things would go better for the rest of the day.

He read the newspaper for twenty minutes and then stood up and lit a cigarette and went out onto his balcony. He looked at his brown arms glowing in the sun, and at his long strong brown hands. His careless hands. He smiled at them affectionately, and leaned over the balcony to flick his ash down into the street below.

Staring up from the dark narrow street was the crippled boy.

Paolo stepped back. He flicked his ash onto the balcony, and wondered what he should do. Twenty minutes ago, when he had come in, he had told himself he should have challenged the boy. Now, again, he realized that he couldn't, or didn't want to. There would be something distasteful in talking to a creature like that. He didn't want to get near him.

It occurred to him to call the police. But what could he say? And if he did call them and they came and asked the boy what he was doing, what would happen? Either he would give some plausible explanation or he would be carted off to a psychiatric home for a checkup, and then released.

Forget about him—ignore him. That was the best thing to do. He was harmless enough; one would be able to knock him over with one finger if necessary. Yes—just forget about him.

Paolo went into his bedroom and made some brief telephone calls. Then he put on his bathing shorts under his jeans, and found a towel.

He had just picked up his paper and was starting to look through it again when he heard a car horn in the street below. He went out onto the balcony. It was Elaine's car. He looked up and down the street and could see no sign of the cripple.

Paolo took his towel and went into his hallway and was about to open the door when it occurred to him that the boy might be in the building. He paused, with his hand on the latch. If he was —well, if he was, he *would* talk to him. It was as simple as that.

He opened the door. There was no one on the landing. He

closed the door behind him and started to walk down the stairs.

He met no one. Walking out into the street, he looked around. He couldn't see the cripple. He felt very relieved, and slightly sick. He got into the car and smiled at Elaine.

Elaine looked haggard. Her shoulder-length hair was lank and seemed more gray than black, and there were red lines in her eyes.

Paolo kissed her on the cheek. "We're looking our age this afternoon."

Elaine wrinkled her small, turned-up nose. "Don't joke. Do you realize it's my birthday two weeks from today? Forty-seven. Isn't that terrible?"

"Yes," Paolo said. "And I wasn't joking."

"Pig. It's your fault. I said let's go at midnight and you insisted on staying."

"We were winning so much it would have been a shame to go."

"I suppose. But you didn't have to get up at eight."

"I didn't wake up till my mother called. But if it's any consolation to you, I've had a disgusting morning. After I'd spoken to you I went out to buy the paper and I was followed by a cripple."

"How exciting! What happened?"

"He followed me home and I looked down from the balcony and he was down in the street, looking up at me. He's gone now. But it was sort of unpleasant. That and my mother in one day!"

"You're sure you weren't imagining things?"

"Quite sure."

They drove along the street, into Via Cavour, and down to the Dori Imperiali. Paolo gazed out of the window and wondered whether he would see the boy; but he saw only tourists with cameras, and ordinary-looking Romans. Then he glanced at Elaine, tiny and leaning forward in her seat as she drove, and wondered whether he should tell her about Christopher.

He had been wanting to for a long time. Elaine had adored Christopher, and had been almost angry with Paolo when, in the spring of the previous year, he had told her, "I'm afraid Christopher has to be dropped." Almost angry, but not quite, since anger would have been against the unwritten, unspoken rules of their friendship. But she had wrinkled her nose and said "Oh," and hadn't laughed or smiled when Paolo had said, "Well, he was beginning to act as if he were my brother or something."

They had never mentioned Christopher's name again, and in the months that followed Paolo kept something secret from Elaine for the first time since he had met her. He didn't tell her about Christopher's telephone calls, about Christopher following him in the street, about Christopher spying on him; about Christopher leaving for England; about Christopher returning to Rome a few months later, radiantly happy, to get rid of his apartment and have his furniture sent north. He didn't tell her about the irritation *he* had felt, the irritation that had become a kind of fury when he had seen Christopher, when they had those long talks together. He didn't tell her that Christopher had meant to come to Rome for just two weeks, but had stayed, three, four, six, eight. He didn't tell her that he had wanted Christopher to stay, had *made* Christopher stay—until, at the end of three months, when Christopher's happiness had been replaced by a state of strange, feverish excitement—he had received a letter from him. He didn't tell her that a week later Christopher had died.

Paolo had often been on the point of telling her; and now, sitting in the car beside her, he was again on the verge of doing so. He looked at her. At her bitten fingernails. At her face without makeup—her funny little face between the two lank sheets of graying hair—the face of a bitter mouse, with its small mouth open, and its widely spaced, tiny mouse teeth.

Elaine turned to him and as she did so she turned her hands on the wheel. The car swerved. Paolo raised his eyebrows and put his hand on the wheel. Elaine smiled gaily and said, "What are you staring at me for? I don't look that dreadful, do I?"

"Yes. But I wasn't really staring at you. You know what my mother said on the phone? That old bitch of a grandmother of mine wants to make her money over to me now, before she dies, but she wants an excuse for doing it and said I should get married."

"The old cow. Isn't she a hundred years old?"

"Two."

"So she'll die soon anyway?"

"Yes, that's what I said."

"And even if she doesn't, don't you dare dream of doing it."

"Oh, I wouldn't, don't worry."

"It's really not worth it at any price. When I think of all those hideous years! Uh!"—and she started on a long diatribe against marriage in particular, husbands in general, and her husband —from whom she had been separated for seven years—in particular.

Paolo had heard it all many times before—heard it, in fact, almost every time he saw Elaine, which was at least four times a week. The story of her disastrous marriage was a part of their repertoire; like a dog they walked together, which, though it always went for the same walk, always found new things along the way to sniff and bark at. Elaine always managed to remember—or invent—some incident she had never spoken of before; some new little horror story. And, true or false, the stories were invariably funny.

Today Paolo found it hard to concentrate on what she was saying—something about her husband having forced her to watch a necrophilic cat screwing its dead mate for three hours, which had made her so sick that she had thrown up. He wished she would be quiet and drive. He wanted to tell her about Christopher, or he didn't want to talk at all. But, he realized, he couldn't tell her about Christopher. Because either his tale or her reaction to it would be against their rules.

As she chattered on he knew that everything was going to irritate him today. His mother. His memories of Christopher. The crippled boy. And now Elaine, and their rules of conduct which made it impossible for him to speak of what was on his mind.

He closed his eyes and listened to her lank Bostonian voice. He wondered if her husband really had been so awful. In any case, she shouldn't have left her liberal New England circle to marry a conservative Italian businessman if she hadn't been prepared to suffer the consequences; nor, having tried and failed, feel so disgusted with herself for having failed—yet not for having tried. And then again her particular brand of bohemianism was getting a bit sad now that she was approaching fifty. If staying up till three, drinking too much, and playing poker made her look and feel so wretched, she shouldn't be so eager to be "one of the boys." He opened his eyes. "I'm thinking nasty thoughts about you."

"Oh, what?"

"Oh—" he smiled.

"Do you often?"

"No. Never in fact."

"Why today then?"

"I don't know."

"Do tell me. Has something just occurred to you about me?"

"No. Not really. Just something I've often thought about that always seemed funny before. Today—it doesn't."

"Oh, dear."

"It'll pass."

"What brought this on?"

"I wanted to talk to you about something"—he pulled a face— "serious."

"You'd only regret it tomorrow. Besides, I don't think I'm feeling strong enough today."

"Yes, you're right." He grinned. "If irony fails the world stops."

"Well, I don't know about the world, but I'll stop talking for a while if you like."

He smiled. She *was* right. He would regret it tomorrow if he spoke to her about Christopher. After all, he couldn't tell her the truth. Because he didn't know it. One could never know the truth. At least irony protected one against any delusions on that score. And Elaine was as aware of that as he. So even if she wasn't entirely successful in playing her part as a free spirit—and even if that part had been thrust unwillingly on her—at least she played it unfailingly. Which was more than anyone else he had ever known had done.

"Do you know, my mother still insists on calling me Paul," he said. "It makes me so mad."

They stayed on the beach till five-thirty, when they drove back into town and went to Elaine's apartment.

They poured themselves drinks and sat at her piano and started to play a Mozart symphony transcribed for four hands.

Elaine was normally a competent pianist, if not a brilliant

one, but that evening she seemed unable to play more than five notes without getting lost, stopping, laughing, and sipping her drink. Though this had occasionally happened before, and Paolo had always laughed with her and drunk with her, now, for the second time that day, he became irritated with her. She saw it, and after twenty minutes—they hadn't even finished playing the first movement—she suggested they give it up. Paolo said, "I'm sorry, I don't know what's wrong with me. Why don't we call Guido and Michele and get them to come over?"

"We can play bridge and get some money off them. That'll cheer you up. And it's infallible. They always lose."

They didn't, however. Paolo, with Elaine as a partner, lost more than seven thousand lire before they stopped playing at midnight. He was furious—with himself, and with Elaine, who seemed to find their losing hilarious; who had played, he thought, as if she had been trying to lose.

After he had kissed her on the cheek, and said goodnight, he murmured, "I'll be in a better mood tomorrow. But really this has been one of the worst days of my life. I guess we can go to the beach again tomorrow, to recover from it."

At home, in bed, before turning his light out, he looked at his photographs on the wall and—as always—felt reassured. Come what may, try him who might—his mother, Christopher, skeletal cripples, even Elaine—those images on the wall were what he lived for. Paolo Levin. He was alive, and free for—himself. And he was always going to be free and alive for himself—to live, entirely and completely, his own life. People only formed relationships because they couldn't bear themselves. But he could. Oh, there were one or two things, maybe, he would have changed, but basically he was happy with himself. Very happy indeed. He had more or less everything he could have wanted. He was good-looking, talented, intelligent, healthy, young—he supposed that thirty was still young; in any case, age was only a state of mind, and he felt young—not rich, but always with the means to earn a comfortable living, and had plenty of friends, who were always replaceable. He would always have plenty of friends as long as he never wanted them or needed them—never felt them to be irreplaceable. He supposed people were attracted to him because he was free, and good-looking, talented ... healthy ... intelligent. ...

He turned out the light and fell asleep.

The next day he was awakened by the telephone at eleven. He knew it would be Elaine calling, and it was. They arranged to go to the beach again that afternoon.

He stretched in bed and felt warm and well.

"I guess," he said to Elaine, "that bad days like yesterday are useful very occasionally to make one appreciate all the others more."

After he had taken a shower he put on his blue jeans and a clean white T-shirt. He had some coffee and smoked a cigarette, and then went down to buy the paper.

He was thumbing through a music magazine at the newsdealer's when he became aware of someone looking at him. He didn't have to turn to see who it was. He knew it could only be the cripple. But he did turn, and it was the cripple, and the black eyes in the thin face were staring at him.

Then Paolo saw something else. The boy was dressed in a pair of obviously new blue jeans, and was wearing a white T-shirt, and his long hideously thin arms were very pale and covered in goose bumps. He was shivering.

2

Paolo closed the music magazine. He had to talk to the boy, ask him what he wanted. He looked over his shoulder at the woman behind the counter. She was reading a comic book with a smile on her face.

There was no one else in the shop. He couldn't speak to the boy in there. He didn't want the woman to hear him; didn't want her to witness a scene he felt sure was going to be, for some reason, squalid.

He started to walk out of the shop, then stopped. He realized he hadn't bought the paper. But he didn't want to go back. He

didn't want to see that monster, staring at him. He decided to
walk a little way down the street, talk to the boy, tell him to stop
following him, and then return for the paper. He had just taken
a step forward when from behind him the woman at the counter
called, *"Ha dimenticato il giornale."*

He bowed his head and turned, and put his hands in the
pockets of his jeans, searching for change. But he had none. He
had to take out his wallet and give the woman a note. As he did
so he heard, or saw out of the corner of his eye, the cripple walk
across the shop, go out of the door, and start to walk away. Paolo
looked up and smiled suddenly at the woman and realized that
he was trembling. He took the newspaper and the change for the
note he had given, said *"Grazie,"* and followed the cripple out of
the shop.

He looked up and down, and saw the boy standing, twenty
yards away, waiting for him.

Paolo went toward him. He had taken no more than two or
three steps when the boy smiled—a kind, rather gentle smile, in
spite of the revolting mouth that smiled it—turned, and started
to walk away. Paolo walked after him, and was gaining on him,
when he realized what he was doing, and stopped. He flushed. It
was grotesque! They had changed roles. He was the pursuer now,
and not the pursued. He stood still and watched the boy walking
on, without looking around.

Paolo found himself in front of a butcher's shop. He went
inside quickly and waited until the woman in front of him had
finished being served, and then asked for a steak. He hoped the
cripple would continue on his way without looking around; and
that it would be a long time before he realized he was no longer
being followed—that when he did realize he would simply go on
walking, and vanish, and never be seen again.

Paolo left the butcher's shop with his steak. He couldn't see
the cripple amid the people in the street doing their shopping. He
started to walk up Via Cavour—opposite the direction the boy
had taken. He wondered what to do. He could either go home
and read the paper or go and sit somewhere in the sun.

After a moment or two he decided to do the latter; he wanted
some fresh air, and it was a beautiful morning. Also, he thought,

if the boy decided to go and wait outside his house … But no. That would mean he was running away. He was going to sit outside and read his paper because it was a beautiful morning and he wanted some fresh air. There was no other reason.

He crossed the road and started to walk up the steps under the Borgia palace. He would go and sit in the park at Colle Oppio, and read his paper. He often did. …

He had been sitting for some ten minutes when he lowered his paper. On a bench, not far from him, the cripple was sitting and staring at him.

Paolo looked around at the women sitting on other benches, chatting; the women pushing prams; a man walking his dog; an old tramp lying on his back on the grass; children riding bicycles; children kicking a ball around; children sitting on the concrete path playing with some colored glass marbles. Everyone seemed intent on his or her activity.

Paolo got up and walked across to the bench where the cripple was sitting and sat down next to him. The boy smiled at him; the same kind smile he had smiled before.

"Perché mi stai seguendo?" Paolo said.

The boy looked at him and stopped smiling. He appeared to be puzzled, and gave a little frown. Then he lowered his head and looked embarrassed. He was shivering with cold.

Paolo narrowed his eyes and stared at him. The boy *was* disgusting. He was weak and crippled and obscene. It would have been so satisfying to hit him.

"Ho chiesto," Paolo began again, quietly and angrily. But he got no further. Because even as he had started speaking the boy had stood abruptly up and started to walk, or rather hop, away, his left leg swinging absurdly inside the stiff new jeans.

Paolo wanted to run after him, to stop him, to hit him. But he looked around the sunny, crowded park, and knew that he couldn't. However, he reasoned with himself, now that he had shown himself to be antagonistic, he would probably see the boy no more.

But he did. An hour and a half later, leaning over his balcony, looking down to see if Elaine had come—he had heard a car horn

—he saw the boy standing in the street, looking up at him.

There was no one else passing in the street at that moment —the car hadn't been Elaine's—and without knowing quite why he did it he spat down in the boy's direction. No sooner had he done so than he felt disgusted with himself, and hoped that the spit wouldn't, by any unfortunate chance, hit its target. But as he watched, the boy moved forward and stepped to one side—and then raised his hand to his face and started to rub it, with a circular motion. He continued to do this for about ten seconds, and finally stopped with his hand covering his mouth and eyes. Then he moved back to where he had been standing before, lowered his hand, and looked up once more, as if offering his face for further humiliation.

Paolo stared at him and realized, with horror, that he was excited. Just for a second; then the excitement passed, and only the horror remained.

He went off the balcony, back into the apartment, and sat down. The situation was becoming frightening. There was only one thing to do, after all. Ignore the boy. Completely. Let him follow him if he wanted. Let him watch him. It wouldn't go on for long—a few days, a week or two at the most. Because, he thought, if he didn't ignore him, he was going to become, in some dark perverted way, involved with him. And he didn't want to. He didn't want to get involved with anyone. Above all not with that freak. He looked at the calendar. September 19. His next concert was on the 26th of October. He had been glad, yesterday, that it was more than a month away. Now he wished it were sooner. Perhaps he would start preparing tomorrow in any case.

Schumann, Liszt, and Berg. Yes. Tomorrow he would start committing all those notes to memory—or at least reminding himself of the Liszt and Berg, which he had learned and played before; start getting his hands to obey his brain; start on another journey into those foreign lands, a journey that would end only when he had learned his way around so perfectly that anyone seeing him or hearing him would think he belonged there.

In the car, going to the sea, he told Elaine that the cripple had followed him again that day. He told her about the newsagent, the butcher, the scene in the park. But he didn't tell her what had happened when he had come home; what he had done when he leaned over the balcony; what the boy had done; what he had felt.

When he had finished Elaine said with a smile, "Well, you'll probably never see him again now." She added, half a minute later, "Knowing you, you'll probably miss him."

When they were on the beach Paolo went, once again, through the events of the day. He thought of the cripple's puzzled expression when he had spoken to him, and of the boy getting up and walking away through the women sitting in the sun, through the barking dogs and shouting children, through the children riding bicycles and playing with marbles. He said, "Did I ever tell you how I tried to kill my brother?"

"I thought you succeeded."

"No. He died of meningitis."

"Oh, yes."

"No. This was when we were small. I was seven, I guess; my brother must have been four. I hated him. He was all fat and blond and was always hanging around me—always wanted to go everywhere I went, do everything with me, play with my friends." He was lying on his back. He turned his head to look at Elaine. She had her eyes closed. He was sure he had told her the story before. But it didn't matter. He enjoyed telling it.

"One summer my parents had taken a house up in Michigan on one of the lakes. As soon as we got there I looked around for someplace I could go on my own where my brother couldn't find me. On the third day I found the perfect thing. About a mile or two from our house they were building another house—or they had been building it, and stopped for some reason. It was less than half finished, but there was a kind of flat concrete roof on. I used to go up there—there was a ladder—and then pull the ladder up, and sit and play with toy cars or read or pretend I was playing the piano.

"Then one day I climbed up onto the roof and pulled the ladder up and found a marble. It was my brother's, I was sure. He had been given a whole packet of new ones, and they had strange colors, and this one did too. First of all I couldn't believe that the little rat had followed me and found out my private place. He was so small. But he obviously had, and then I got mad, thinking about it. So one afternoon I told everyone I was going off to play with some kids who lived near. My brother was at home. Then I went off, and came to my unfinished house, climbed up to the roof, but left the ladder in its place.

"About an hour and a half later I hear someone approaching, and sure enough up the ladder puffs my little fat blond brother. He couldn't see me because there was a low wall that divided the roof and I was hiding behind it. After a few minutes I peered over this wall and he had his back to me. He had brought the packet of marbles with him and scattered them on the concrete. I started to climb over the wall quietly. I don't know what I wanted to do. Jump on him, scream at him or something I guess. Give him a shock. But he didn't hear me and I was right behind him and he was about six feet from the edge of the roof—and then I suddenly knew *exactly* what I was going to do. I took a step forward and gave him a great shove. It was like a silent comedy. He shot forward and put his foot on a marble and then another one and reeled off the roof. It was perfect. And it was hilariously funny.

"I guess, logically, he should have fallen over on his face when I pushed him, but—well, it must have been an inspired push. Anyway I just yelled with laughter. And I was sure I had killed him. I meant to. I went to the edge of the roof and looked down, still laughing, and there was the little bastard pulling himself out of some great big bush. It was the only bush anywhere near the house and really big and he'd fallen right into it. He was all scratched and cut, of course, but otherwise completely all right. And if he'd fallen anywhere else he would have been killed, I'm sure—the roof was quite high. But the strange thing was he didn't cry or start screaming. He just looked up at me all sulky and miserable, but—I don't know—somehow satisfied. It made me think that perhaps he *had* heard me creeping up behind him on the roof.

"But then I got terrified—I was sure my parents would beat me, lock me up, send me away to prison—God knows what. Anyway, I ran down the ladder and grabbed his hand and walked him home and I was crying and trembling and he didn't say a word all the way. When we got near the house I heard my mother shouting—and she never does that, she's usually very patient and quiet. I shouted back and when she saw my brother all cut and scratched she rushed toward us and started screaming where had he been, she'd been going frantic looking for him, etc. And she didn't even ask how he'd got so messed up. After a while she calmed down and took him upstairs and patched him up and put him to bed. I hung around the whole time to hear what he said to her. But he didn't say a word. So when my mother had finished with him and we were alone I told her the kids I'd gone to play with hadn't been home so I'd gone for a walk through the woods and I heard someone following me and found it was him—my brother—and I'd told him he was very bad and he started to run away from me and fell down a bank into a bush.

"He never did tell my mother the truth, but he never forgot what I'd done, and never followed me again. When my mother wrote and told me he'd died so suddenly, my first thought was thank God he'll never be able to tell them now. His death sort of ensured my innocence."

Paolo paused. He felt sleepy. He said, "The only thing I never understood was how he'd managed to go to that house the first time—or however many times he went—without my mother noticing that he'd gone. It was only that last time—and then it was nearly too late." He smiled, and rolled over, and looked at Elaine. She was asleep.

"You didn't hear my story," he said to her an hour later, when they were both awake.

"I know, I'm sorry. I heard the beginning. You can tell me some other time. Talking of which, what were you going to tell me yesterday and then you wouldn't?"

"Nothing."

"Yes you were. You were going to tell me something serious."

"Oh, that. But you said you didn't want to hear."

"Well, I do now. I'm feeling mellow."

Paolo looked up at the blue sky. He thought of himself laughing on the roof of the unfinished house as his brother went flying off. That hadn't been serious. Only his guilt had been. And he'd never been found guilty.

"It doesn't seem so serious today."

"So you'll tell me?"

"Yes. If you like."

"Well?"

"You remember Christopher?"

"Yes, of course."

"He killed himself."

"Oh."

There was a long silence, and Elaine propped herself up on her elbows and looked down toward the sea. Paolo watched her. She screwed up her little mouse face as if she were making some great effort. Finally, still gazing at the sea, she came out with, "How stupid."

Then she looked at Paolo with a frown and said, "What on earth for?"

"God knows."

"How bloody stupid." Then, "Poor Christopher. When?"

"Six months ago."

"Did you only find out yesterday? Is that why you were so strange?"

"No, I knew the day it happened."

"Oh," Elaine said again. "Why didn't you tell me before?"

"I don't know. I've often wanted to. But I always thought it was serious. I just realized now that it isn't. It's just—bloody stupid, as you said."

"How did he do it?"

"Shot himself."

"How horrible. Where did it happen?"

"Here in Rome. In his apartment. It was in all the papers."

"You know I never look at a paper."

"I know. And when you didn't say anything about it I guessed you hadn't seen or heard anything, so—I don't know. I felt sort of guilty about it. That's why I never told you. I thought you might blame me in some way."

"Why should you feel guilty?"

"Oh, because we were both very friendly with him, weren't we? Then we—I—decided he"—Paolo gave a small smile—"had to go. I've always half thought that you might say I shouldn't have decided that."

"But that was a year before, wasn't it? You hadn't seen him since, had you?"

"No."

"Well, then. People don't kill themselves because they had a fight with a friend months and months before. There must have been something else—something that happened in that year when we didn't know him any more. But still it's silly, because I'm sure people only kill themselves nine times out of ten so that other people will feel sorry for them or feel guilty about them. Like you do. But there's not much satisfaction in that if you're dead. But I am sorry. Christopher was nice wasn't he?" She shivered. "I think I wish you hadn't told me."

They lay down again on the warm sand.

Paolo said, "When does school start again?"

"The second of October."

"Looking forward to it?"

"No. The summer holidays are so long I get out of the habit. The idea of getting up early every morning and facing all those little horrors day after day is awful. I wish I could do something else besides teach."

They didn't talk any more for a while. Paolo closed his eyes and remembered thinking that either his telling Elaine about Christopher's death, or her reaction, would have been against the rules. But he hadn't really told her about Christopher's death, so her reaction wasn't the one he'd imagined. It wasn't a genuine reaction. Or perhaps it was. Perhaps the fact that she didn't know about all those other months didn't change anything. Christopher's death had been stupid. That was all. Christopher was stupidly dead, and Paolo was innocent. He'd thought that Elaine might blame him. But he was innocent. He'd only just realized it as he'd been telling the story about his brother.

He thought of himself laughing on the roof of the unfinished house as his brother went flying off. He thought of Christopher's stupid death. Everything was a comedy. One had to live and die comically. Because in comedies no one was guilty, and in tragedies everyone was. Yes. He repeated it to himself. Everything was a comedy. He thought of the children in the park that morning, playing with marbles. He thought of the cripple. Though he tried, he somehow couldn't make the cripple come under the heading of comic.

That evening Elaine was busy, so Paolo had dinner with some friends. He was home by midnight, and went to bed immediately. He woke at nine, and wondered whether he should get up and go down and buy his newspaper now. But he decided not to. He would go down at the usual time and buy the paper, and after he had had lunch he would start practicing.

He took a book from his bedside table and started reading.

At eleven Elaine called and told him that the day was cloudy and windy and not very warm. They talked for a while, and agreed to phone each other the following day.

Paolo got up and dressed—in spite of what Elaine had told him about the weather—in his usual uniform of T-shirt and jeans. He looked at his strong brown arms and smiled. The cripple would freeze today.

He went down to buy his paper and the boy was at his usual place, looking through magazines. Paolo ignored him but, standing near, could hear his teeth chattering. He felt pleased. He glanced to see what the boy was looking at. It was a physique and body-building magazine. Paolo smiled.

He bought some food and went home and the cripple followed him around the shops, and then stationed himself in the street under the apartment.

After he had eaten and washed the dishes, Paolo went to the piano and began to play. As he did so, he heard a roll of thunder and, looking out of the window, saw that it was starting to rain. He left the piano and went out onto the balcony and looked down. The cripple was pressed against the wall of the building opposite.

He watched him for a while as the rain began to fall more heavily, but the boy didn't move, and Paolo felt, as he had the day before when he had spat at him, excited. Only today the excitement didn't pass after a second. It stayed with him, even after he had come in off the balcony, out of the rain, and closed the windows. It excited him to think of that deformed skeleton down there, shivering in the street, waiting for him. Waiting *on* him. He looked at the Liszt sonata in front of him and began, again, to play. But he couldn't concentrate. He played for ten minutes, and made so many mistakes that he stopped, irritated. He smoked a cigarette, and then tried again. But there seemed to be no communication between his eyes, his brain, and his hands. After half an hour he gave up. There was something blocking him. And he knew that that something was the idea of the cripple, down there in the rain. The excitement he had felt changed to anger. He remembered how Christopher had had the same talent for disturbing him; Christopher telephoning at the wrong moment, dropping by unexpectedly, making it impossible for him to play.

He smoked another cigarette and considered what to do. If he was unable to ignore the boy, and couldn't talk to him—he had tried that yesterday in the park to no avail—he had to do something else. There must be some other way to shake him off. He thought for a while, and then had an idea.

He went into his bedroom and put on a sweater and a thick pair of shoes. He took his umbrella and left the apartment. He ran down the stairs and out into the street. The storm had been brief and the rain had almost stopped. He saw the boy huddled in a doorway. He went toward him, drew level with him, and walked past him without looking at him.

He walked down to the Fori Imperiali before turning to check that he was being followed. He was. But he felt no satisfaction. It seemed to him that what was happening now was inevitable and out of his control.

He walked to the Piazza Venezia and along the Corso to the Piazza del Popolo. He climbed the hill up to the Pincio. The cripple followed. Paolo thought of that one good leg hopping along. It must be very strong. But however strong it was, it wasn't as strong as the two legs of Paolo Levin. It would have to give out eventually. Or if the leg didn't, the body would. That thin shivering body in its wet cotton T-shirt. Paolo looked at his watch. Three-thirty. He could, and would, keep walking till eight tonight if necessary. He would keep walking until the cripple gave up.

He walked through the Villa Borghese and down Via Veneto, along Via Bissolati, and eventually to the station. The boy followed. From the station he walked to Santa Maria Maggiore, and then down to San Giovanni. The boy followed. Paolo began to feel tired, and panicky. The boy wasn't human.

At six o'clock Paolo went into a bar and called Elaine. He said, "Hey, listen, I'm having the most grotesque afternoon. You know that cripple I told you about? Well, he's been following me now for two and a half hours. I went out for a walk and he started following and I decided to keep on until he stopped, but he hasn't. I'm exhausted. I don't know what to do. I don't think he's going to stop."

"Are you all right, Paolo?" Elaine said, with only a trace of humor.

"Yes, of course I'm all right. I just don't know how to shake off this freak who's following me."

"Well, don't be stupid. Go home. What do you care if he does follow you? He doesn't harm you, does he?"

"No, but—"

"Oh, come on," Elaine repeated. "I mean—listen, if you went out for a walk I guess you wanted this boy to follow you, so I don't know why you're complaining now. Go *home*. It can't worry you if he's out in the street."

"It does, though."

"Oh, Paolo!" Elaine laughed. "What's wrong with you? You should be pleased. The boy's obviously in love with you."

"Well, what am I going to do?"

"Nothing. I've told you. Go home. Ignore him. Or if you really do like him following you, keep on walking." She laughed again.

"You're no help."

"Well, what am I supposed to say?"

"I don't know."

"I've told you what to do. Have you tried talking to him?"

"Yes, I tried yesterday. I told you."

"Try again today."

"No. There's no point. He'd just hop off and wait twenty yards away."

"Do you want to get in a taxi and come over here and have a drink?"

"Yes, but I'm not going to. I've got to do something about this. I've got to stop it."

"Go to the police."

"I can't. That would be—I don't know."

"Well, listen, dear, you do what you want, and call me later to tell me what's happened."

"Are you going to be in tonight?"

"Till about nine. Then I'm going out to dinner with my new lover."

"Who is he?"

"I'm only joking."

"And even if you weren't—"

"I wouldn't tell you."

"I'll talk to you later. *Ciao.*"

"*Ciao.*"

After he had hung up, Paolo wondered why he had called Elaine. She had been no help, and had he thought about it before he would have realized that she couldn't have been. He wished he hadn't called. The cripple was something to do with him, and only him. The cripple was something unspeakable and foreign; something to do with misery and guilt and unhappiness and love; something to do with a world that wasn't his. Elaine kept all sorts of secrets from him, he was sure; she didn't tell him all the messy affairs she had, or all about those she did mention. She didn't tell him about the boring Anglo-American school where she taught piano and violin; about her money problems. And while he had never kept anything secret from her apart from the business about Christopher, it was only because he ordered his life so well, kept it all within the bounds of his own created world, that he had nothing to hide. He had nothing that couldn't be brought out into the open and laughed at—nothing except, now, this cripple who had blundered in and, for some reason, couldn't be neutralized with irony and laughter.

Paolo left the bar. The cripple was leaning against a wall some distance away. His face was gray. Paolo stood on the sidewalk and decided that he would, though it would be useless, try to talk to him once more. But just as he decided, and before he could even take a step in the boy's direction, the cripple suddenly raised his hand and went hopping into the street. A taxi stopped. The boy got in, and the taxi drove off. As it went past him, Paolo saw that the cripple, sitting in the back of the yellow car, was smiling.

He went back inside the bar and ordered a brandy. He was tired and humiliated. He told himself that he had won; that the boy had given up and gone home. But he knew it wasn't so. *He* had given up. He had decided to walk and walk until the cripple dropped with fatigue; instead of which he had changed his mind. He had weakened; he had been going to talk to the boy, to threaten him or reason with him. And the second he had made that decision the boy had seen the weakness in his face, and known that the victory, at least for that day, was his. Meanwhile Paolo was stuck in a bar somewhere, drinking brandy, which he didn't like, and was tired. He had wasted a whole afternoon.

He took a taxi home. He didn't answer the phone when it rang, and didn't call Elaine. He didn't want to talk to her. He lay on his bed and looked at the photographs of himself, and the posters of his concerts; at the images and evidence of his brilliance, of his great technical achievement, of his creation; of himself, Paolo Levin.

He listened to a concert on the radio and at nine went out to a restaurant. After he had eaten he went to the cinema.

Next morning Elaine told him on the phone that the weather was fine and warm again, and suggested that they go to the beach; it would be one of their last opportunities that year. But Paolo said no—he had meant to practice yesterday, and he hadn't been able to. Today he would. Elaine tried to reason with him, and he almost snapped at her. "No, I'm going to practice."

He spent the whole afternoon at the piano, and refused to allow himself to get up and leave it. But he played badly. He played disastrously. He sounded like Elaine playing when she was very drunk. He knew the notes he had to play; knew the value and the color he had to give them; he knew exactly what the composer had written; but he couldn't express what he knew.

He didn't go out onto his balcony and look down. He didn't have to. He was certain the cripple was there. He had been at the newsagent's as usual that morning, and now was waiting in the street. He didn't have to look, and didn't want to. He wouldn't be weak. He wouldn't even acknowledge the cripple's existence. He *would* practice. The cripple was nothing to him. No one was anything to him, except Paolo Levin.

At six o'clock he gave up. He went to lie down on his bed. He looked at his photographs, and felt that the cripple was breathing on the glass that covered them, dimming their brilliance.

That evening he stayed in and read Proust. He unplugged his telephone.

Next morning on the phone Elaine said, "Paolo, I'm beginning to get worried about you. I wish you'd stop this nonsense. You're getting miserable."

"Yes, I know. But what am I supposed to do?"

"*Do* call the police."

"It'd be no use. They'd only warn him, or maybe take him off somewhere for psychiatric tests, and then they'd let him out and he'd come back. I know."

"But why does he bother you so much?"

"I don't know."

"Can I come around this afternoon and see him?"

"I'd rather you didn't!"

"Well, when am I going to see *you?*"

"Look—I'll call you. I'm sorry to be so difficult, but until this is over I can't really think about anything else. It's turning into a nightmare."

"You don't want to come and stay with me?"

"No. Why should I run away from him?"

"Well, if he upsets you that much—"

"And anyway, I can't stay away forever, can I? And I'm sure he'd find out where I was staying if I did go somewhere."

He couldn't practice that afternoon, and he couldn't sleep that night, until at three o'clock he took a sleeping pill.

Elaine woke him at eleven. He said, "Look, I'm sorry, but I took a pill and I'm still asleep and I'll call you back."

He didn't, though. He had told her the day before that he'd be in touch with her; in other words, not to call him. But she had wakened him. He felt dreadful. And he couldn't go back to sleep.

The cripple waited again that day, and Paolo still couldn't practice. He went to bed at ten and took another sleeping pill.

Next morning Elaine said on the phone, "Look, Paolo, I'm not just going to be forgotten about until you've decided what to do about your pet freak."

Paolo wanted to put the phone down without replying. But he said very quietly, "I'm sorry, but I have asked you to leave me alone until I've sorted this out. Don't you realize I've just had it? I don't want to see anyone and I can't sleep at night and—oh, for God's sake have a bit of *tact*."

"Paolo, we are supposed to be friends, and I just want to help."

She was pleading with him, and the tone of her voice sickened him. She couldn't help. She was only good for laughing. A laughing bitter Bostonian mouth. She was as crippled as the boy down in the street.

"If you want to help, please leave me alone for a while." He spoke very slowly, as if reasoning with a child or a madman. "I'm sorry," he added, crossly.

"Well, we have been friends for four years now. I think I have some rights—"

"I'll call you next week. Goodbye."

Trembling, he put the phone down. Stupid little woman. How dare she talk about rights. He lay in bed and smoked a cigarette. He told himself to be calm. There was no point in upsetting himself further. He told himself that he should be pleased, as Elaine had said two days ago, or at least amused, that the cripple was down there all the time, waiting for him. He should consider the whole affair a perverse game he had never played before, and he enjoyed games, and usually won. He had been excited when he had spat at the boy, and then again when he had seen him pressed against the wall, shivering under the rain. He shouldn't have struggled against that excitement, or been horrified by it. He should have indulged it. He should go down now and spit right in the boy's face. He should think up elaborate tortures.

He didn't convince himself. Because the boy was so ugly, so

foul, the excitement he had generated those times had been ugly and foul. It hadn't been pleasant. It had been degrading. It had been serious.

Serious. The word kept on repeating itself to him. That was what was so terrible about the cripple. He was serious. And nothing must be serious. It was because people's ideas and beliefs became serious that wars broke out, that there was misery and unhappiness in the world.

Christopher had tried to be serious, and other people, on other occasions—but Paolo had always overcome them. He had always managed to emerge from the ordeal with his creation, Paolo Levin, intact. Paolo Levin—the creator of himself, and of the comic world. He would emerge victorious this time, too. His creation would not be destroyed. He would find a way of making the cripple just another character in the comedy. He wouldn't allow him to act in a tragedy—or, worse, step across the footlights and threaten him, the author of the work itself.

He smiled in his bed. If anyone could have heard his thoughts he would have been considered insane. But even if he thought of himself and the cripple in less grandiose terms, the boy *was* interfering with his normally very pleasant life and had to be stopped. And he couldn't cope with Elaine if she was going to start feeling bitter and insulted because he wanted to have a week off, as it were, from their friendship. Still, he could make his peace with her later.

He began to feel calmer, and eventually decided he would invite the boy up to his apartment, and talk to him pleasantly.

When he went to the newsagent's, the boy wasn't there. Paolo hung around the shop for longer than usual, waiting for him; but he didn't come. He did his shopping; no one followed him. He had his lunch, and looked down from his balcony; there was no one standing in the street.

He felt very slightly disappointed. But then he decided that the boy must have given him the day off on purpose, so that he could relax. Paolo called a friend of his who came around with his car, and they drove to Bracciano together, and Paolo took some photographs of the lake, and got his friend to take some of him.

"You're insane, you know that," the friend said with a laugh as he gave the camera back.

Paolo smiled. "Yes, I know. But other people keep diaries."

He went to bed at one, and was sure he would sleep well. But when he closed his eyes he started thinking about the cripple. He wondered what it must be like to grow up deformed. What the boy must have thought as he followed him around, as he stood for hours in the street. What sort of family the boy had, and what sort of life he led normally. Perhaps he often followed people around, until he taunted them into spitting at him, or beating him up, or having him arrested. Perhaps that was what he liked. Paolo wondered why he hadn't come that day.

He did eventually fall asleep, but his dreams were full of the cripple and he kept on waking up, and in the morning he felt as if he hadn't slept. He had an idea that the day before had been the lull before the storm.

The cripple smiled at him in the newsagent's, as if to apologize for not having come the day before. Paolo didn't acknowledge the smile.

That afternoon it rained heavily and steadily, and Paolo didn't even go to the piano. He didn't want to know whether he could play or not. He was frightened of hearing himself. He sat in his armchair staring out of the window until three o'clock, and then put on a raincoat and took his umbrella. He felt very calm. This was the end. There would be no more following, no more vain attempts to speak to the boy, no more hopping away. Today was going to be decisive.

He went downstairs and out into the street. The boy was still wearing only a T-shirt and jeans. He was standing in a doorway. Paolo walked toward him staring at the wet cobbles, as if he were going to walk past him. But as he drew level with him he stopped, turned, and looked up. The boy drew back into the doorway; Paolo followed him. The boy retreated, down a dark passage, his black eyes lowered, his wide wet lips trembling. Paolo followed him down the passage, to the foot of a worn dark staircase.

"*Senti*," he said. His voice was husky, and quiet, and he cleared his throat.

The boy looked past him, as if searching for a way of escape. Paolo could smell garlic on his breath.

Paolo repeated, "*Senti*." His voice was still husky.

The boy suddenly laughed, and said very quickly, in a deep, soft voice, "I wish to God you'd speak English. I don't understand a word of Italian." He had a slight American accent.

Paolo stared at him. He felt so confused he didn't know what to do. It had never occurred to him ... then he flushed, and the idea that the boy was American, and wasn't some sort of Italian, or foreigner, made him feel so angry that he thought he would kill him.

"What the fuck have you been following me around for, you little freak?" he hissed.

The boy narrowed his eyes and bowed his face—he was taller than Paolo—until it was only about a foot away from Paolo's. The wide lips were no longer trembling; in fact, the boy looked joyfully confident. He said, enunciating each word very clearly, "What the fuck do you think I've been following you around for? I'm in love with you."

Paolo took a step back. He couldn't stand that smell of garlic. He forced himself to speak calmly. "You can be in love with me or not," he said. "But you're going to stop following me around or I'll call the police or I'll beat your face in."

The boy shook his head slowly and smiled. "You won't call the police, and if you beat me up I'll call for help, and you see what people do to you for beating up a cripple." As he said the last word his thin arms shot up and pushed Paolo, who, not expecting the move, and caught off balance, fell over. The boy hopped past him and went out into the street. Paolo was picking himself up when the boy turned his head and called back, "Besides, you might hurt your hands." Then he went hopping off.

Paolo ran down the passage after him. But when he got to the street he remembered what the boy had said, and realized he was right. He couldn't start beating him up in public.

The boy hopped along in the rain. He wasn't trying to escape. He was going somewhere. Paolo followed, keeping ten yards or so behind. He didn't know what he was doing; he couldn't think. He only knew that he had to follow the boy, and when they eventually reached their destination—then he would see. He would talk to the boy, or hit the boy, or kill the boy. He would do something—whatever had to be done.

They walked up to Via Nazionale, and under the Traforo; as they were going through the dripping white-tiled tunnel, through the black fumes of the cars and buses, through the noise of motors racing and horns blowing, Paolo felt that he was being led, as in some religious tragedy, into damnation.

3

The cripple kept walking at the same speed until he was halfway up Via Francesco Crispi. His soaked T-shirt was transparent, and his mass of brown curly hair seemed to have solidified on his head. Then, suddenly, he started running, his bad leg swinging in odd arcs as the other leg pumped up and down. He sprang along, ran over Via Sistina, up the hill, and disappeared into a doorway. Paolo followed, but he was nearly hit by a car at the crossing, and by the time he got to the doorway the boy was out of sight. He saw that there was an elevator, and it was in use, and he watched the red light that indicated the floors. The elevator stopped at the fifth. The red light went out, and Paolo started to walk up the stairs. He wanted time to compose himself.

When he reached the fifth floor—it was the top—he paused. There were two doors off the landing. Only one had a bell, though there was no name on it. He wondered what he was going to do. He told himself that he felt grim and implacable, but he didn't. He wished he could go home. He pressed the bell.

He heard someone coming to the door. He lowered his head, and then raised it. When the boy opened the door he would walk straight in. He must keep in charge of the situation.

But the boy didn't open the door; a girl did. Confused, Paolo took a step back. He muttered, "*Mi dispiace, ho sbagliato,*" and indicated with his head the other door, and turned toward it. As he did, the girl said in a soft deep voice—in English—"That door doesn't go anywhere. It leads out onto the roof." Paolo realized that she was tall and slim and had a mass of brown curly hair and very dark eyes that seemed black.

He turned back toward her. She looked at him as if sizing him up, and said, "You must be Paolo." Then she smiled gravely and corrected herself. "I mean, you *are* Paolo, aren't you? Please come in." She had a slight American accent, and she spoke at once apologetically and decisively.

Paolo said nothing, but went through the door the girl held open for him. She closed it behind him, took his raincoat and umbrella, and laid them on a small red velvet chair. Then she led him across the shining marble floor of the hall, and into a living room. A big light room with eighteenth-century furniture.

"Would you like a drink?"

"A Scotch, please."

He said it without thinking; but having said it he felt angry with himself. The girl had managed—as his mother always managed—to put him on the defensive. He had come to attack, to demand an explanation; and instead he had slipped quite easily into the position of one who makes a social call of no importance. But then he thought that perhaps this was not only natural, but also for the best. One had to neutralize the dangerous, defuse the explosive; smile and accept a drink and pretend that the world, and everything in it, was normal. All human intercourse was a comedy of manners; it would be useless and false to treat it as a tragedy. Still, though it was only a small one, the girl had won the first point.

She went over to a cabinet and started pouring out drinks. With her back turned she said, "Do sit down, please."

Paolo sat on a small silk gray and gold chair, and again he had a moment of anger. It was as if he had come to be interviewed for a job. Once more, he checked himself. It didn't matter who gained the first points. He would win the game in the end.

The girl, who was dressed in a black sweater and black skirt, came over to him and handed him a glass; she held another, for herself, in a hand that was gripping so tightly that the knuckles were white. She looked just like the crippled boy, only she wasn't crippled; she was rather beautiful, in fact. She wasn't as thin as

the boy, and Paolo noticed that under her black sweater she had
an enormous bosom, which looked out of proportion to the rest
of her body. She walked with her shoulders slightly hunched, as
if trying to minimize it, or apologize for it. She wore no makeup,
and her face was pale and strained. "My name's Maggie," she
said. When she spoke her jaw moved to one side, giving her wide
mouth a strange, ironical twist.

She sat down opposite Paolo and bowed her head and sipped
her drink. "Maggie Parsons," she said. She looked up at Paolo,
and then down again at her glass. She went on very quickly. "My
brother's name is Ralph, but it isn't really, he's called Randolph
and I guess I'm Marjorie, but we sort of changed our names a
few years back—for our European experience—you know." She
stopped, and continued to stare into her glass.

Paolo took some cigarettes from the pocket of his jeans and
offered them to the girl. She took one. Paolo said, "I'm sorry, I
don't have a light."

"There's a lighter on the table there." The girl nodded toward
a tiny table by her chair, and Paolo wondered why she didn't
take the lighter herself. But he picked it up and lit it and held the
flame in front of her. She lifted her head slightly, though she kept
her eyes lowered, and as she put the cigarette to her mouth and
moved it toward the lighter he saw that her hand was shaking
so violently she was having difficulty making contact with the
flame. She was, he realized, terrified.

Then they both sat in silence. Paolo looked around the big
room. There were doors at either end; one he had come through,
from the hall. The other, he presumed, led to bedrooms, bath-
rooms, and, somewhere, the cripple.

"Ralph's changing," Maggie said. "He was soaked. I told him
to have a bath and put on dry clothes." She finally looked up and
stared, almost accusingly, at Paolo's jeans and T-shirt. "You're not
wet at all, are you? Can I get you a towel or something?"

"No, I'm fine."

There was another moment of silence, which they both broke
at the same time; both said, "I'm sorry."

"How did you know my name?" Paolo asked.

"We saw your recital in Milan last Monday."

"Oh." A long pause. "But you live here in Rome?"

"I don't know. I mean yes. Now. But we only arrived that Tuesday—the day after your concert." A pause. "We came down and I found this apartment the same day. I was lucky, I think. It's very expensive, of course, and this furniture isn't really very comfortable, but it'll do for a while. I've taken it for three months. It'll give us a chance to look around, and I didn't want to take an unfurnished place until we've decided whether we like it here. See what we're going to do. You know." She looked Paolo in the eye, as if what they were going to do depended on him.

Paolo wondered how he could get the conversation around to the cripple.

"Where've you come from?" he said.

"We've been living in London for the last ten years. We went there when I was fourteen." She seemed embarrassed.

Paolo had thought she was older. "What did you do in London when you were fourteen?"

"Went to school. My father was working for an American company that opened a factory in England. They made brake linings. He was there for five years. By that time I was nineteen and had a flat of my own and a job, and when he went back to Detroit, Ralph and I stayed on." She was still speaking quickly, and apologetically.

"How old is—?" He couldn't bring himself to say "Ralph."

"Twenty-one."

There was another long silence, and Paolo thought that perhaps now he could start asking the questions he had to ask. But he said, "You know, that's like me. I came to Italy when I was fourteen. I enrolled in the Conservatorio here and went to school. I lived with a family until I was seventeen and then took a place by myself."

"Yes," Maggie said.

Paolo wasn't sure what she meant by that, so he went on, "I used to go back to the States every summer to see my family. But then three years ago they came to live here themselves. They live in Stresa—up on Lago Maggiore."

"Yes," Maggie repeated. Then she smiled and said, "We know." Before Paolo could ask how she knew, she said, "Did you know

Italian when you came here? I mean, wasn't it difficult going to school?"

"My mother taught me some Italian. She was born here. Then I picked it up pretty quickly when I arrived. But I went to an Anglo-American school, besides the Conservatorio."

Maggie nodded, and Paolo wondered if she had known all that too. But he didn't want to stop this awkward, formal conversation now. With every moment it was becoming more difficult for him to ask what he wanted to ask. He said hurriedly, "You know, by a freak of chance I was born in Italy, too. During the war. My father was a doctor here, with the army. My mother was a nurse." He smiled. "She didn't tell anyone she was pregnant, and she's normally quite big so apparently no one noticed, or if they did they didn't say anything—and I was born prematurely. They got married three months later." A pause. "I don't look as if I was a premature baby, do I? We're supposed to be weak and sickly all our lives. And I was almost three months premature."

Maggie looked at him; looked at his body. "No," she said vaguely.

"But I was lucky to be born here, because it meant I was able to get dual nationality, so I can work here fairly regularly without any difficulty."

They were talking like two people who had met, for the first time, at a party, and didn't want to have to think whether they liked each other. But they were not at a party, and he *had* to ask about Ralph.

"How do you know about me?" He tried to make the question sound casual.

Maggie frowned slightly. "It's not very hard to find out about people."

Paolo waited for her to go on, but she didn't. He looked at her, but she avoided his eyes. It wasn't true, he thought. It was very hard to find out about people. Perhaps she was lying. She had listened to him talk, and then said she knew. To interest him, maybe, or to puzzle him. He hoped she was lying. He didn't like to think that cripple knew all about him.

He looked down at his glass and said, "Do you know that your brother has been following me around for a week now? Every morning—and then he waits outside my apartment, and—"

"Yes, I know," Maggie said.

"Do you know why? I mean—I guess it's stupid, but it worries me and I can't practice and then I get irritated with myself and—"

"Hasn't he told you why?"

"No. I mean—" He stopped. He looked at the girl, and wondered if he could tell her that her brother had said that he loved him. "Yes," he said.

"Well, then?" Maggie smiled.

"He said—" He couldn't say it.

"He thinks he loves you."

Paolo nodded. He murmured, "Well—?"

"Well, I expect he does."

They sat in silence.

"But—"

"But?"

"It's grotesque."

"Yes, I suppose it is."

"Do you think if you asked him not to—?"

"No," Maggie said.

"What do you mean?"

"I mean if I asked him not to he wouldn't listen to me, and anyway I wouldn't dream of asking him. He's old enough to know what he wants to do."

Paolo stared at her. She was beautiful, with her pale face and dark eyes and her jaw that slipped to one side when she spoke. But perhaps she was mad, like her brother.

"Please ask him to stop," he said. "I can't do anything with him there."

Maggie stood up. "No," she said. She sounded, suddenly, very angry. "I will not ask him to stop and if you get irritated with yourself because he's waiting in the street outside your house that's your concern. It's nothing to do with me or Ralph."

"I'll have to call the police if it goes on."

"Oh, call the fucking police," Maggie snapped. She sounded hysterical. She must be mad. Brother and sister. They didn't know anything about him apart from his name, and they probably only knew that because they had come to his recital.

He stood up and faced her. "Well, I guess there's no point in my staying."

Maggie turned away from him and murmured, "No." She sounded as if she were about to start crying. Paolo looked at her back, her hunched shoulders. "I'm sorry," she whispered.

He sighed and said, "Well, if you're sorry why don't you, or won't you, do something?"

"Because"—Maggie turned to him, frowning again—"I don't want to sound stupid, but what I mean is—I feel sorry for you. How can anyone who's supposed to be intelligent and civilized get so upset when someone tells them that they love them? What's so awful in that?"

Now Paolo felt angry. "Oh, for Christ's sake." He tried to keep his voice down. "That's not just stupid, that's"—he remembered what Elaine had said about Christopher's death—"bloody stupid. Don't talk such crap. You know what I mean."

"Yes. I know what you mean but *you* don't know what I mean, obviously. Tell me, what is so wrong with someone saying they love you, or even actually being in love with you?"

"For Christ's sake," Paolo said again. "Stop being so infantile. I don't know your brother and I don't want to know him and I don't want him to follow me about and I don't want him to say he loves me. It's sick."

"Oh!" Maggie cried. "Sick! Who's talking?" She looked as if she were going to hit him.

Paolo started to walk toward the door. The scene was getting to be like something out of a bad film. He went into the hall and put on his raincoat. Maggie followed him and watched him.

He said, "Please tell your brother that he disgusts me and that if I see him following me again I shall go to the police and have him taken off to a madhouse."

"You do what you want and we'll do what we want." She paused. "But how come if you're so disgusted with the idea of someone being in love with you, you can go and stare at all those photographs of yourself? How come you go out and get your friends to take photographs of you? Why don't you go to the police about yourself?"

Paolo put his umbrella back on the red velvet chair. He whispered, "How the fuck do you know about my photographs? Has that little freak been into my apartment somehow?"

Maggie picked up his umbrella and handed it to him. She said, quite calmly, "Have you ever not been disgusted with someone who told you that they loved you?"

She was a stupid, infantile prig. "No. No one," he said, and opened the front door.

"Well, I feel sorry for you."

"You feel how you like."

As he went out onto the landing Maggie said, "You're a fool. I'm warning you—and I'm quite serious—if you do go to the police, or if you touch Ralph, or harm him in any way, he'll kill you. And there's no point in trying to run away from him. We've got plenty of money now. He'll follow you. You couldn't get him locked up all his life. He'd follow you all over the world."

Paolo looked around him. At the quiet clean landing. At the tall beautiful girl dressed in black, with her large bosom. He looked down at the floor. She had meant what she had said.

"But why? What've I done? Why me? Why doesn't he follow someone else? Why doesn't he fall in love with someone else?"

Maggie lowered her head. "He did once."

"And?"

"And the person tried to get away."

"And?"

"And he died."

"You're crazy," Paolo whispered. "Both of you."

Maggie looked up at him and smiled. "No, we're not. We just want—" She paused as if she were trying to remember something. Then she gave up the effort and added weakly, ". . . to live. We want to do something worthwhile. I guess we're kind of old-fashioned."

They were crazy. "But why *me*? When did this happen?"

"Ralph fell in love with you when he saw you at your concert." She laughed suddenly.

"But *why*? Just physically?"

"No. Oh, sure, that too. But—" She shrugged. "Well, if you think we're crazy I might as well tell you everything. Ralph wants to save you. And if he can't—if you won't let him"—she paused, and smiled—"well, I don't want to sound melodramatic, but if you don't let him, you're damned. He *will* kill you. But he can save you, you know. If you'll let him."

Paolo shook his head wonderingly. "I'm supposed to let him save me from—him?"

"I guess you could put it like that," Maggie said. She smiled again. "It does sound sort of crazy, you're right. But it's not. Please believe me. He *will* kill you. He hasn't got much to lose, poor baby."

"And what am I supposed to do?"

"Oh, don't worry. Leave it to him."

The girl came right up to him, and appeared to be studying his face. She said, "I'm sorry our first meeting has been so—unnatural." She leaned forward and kissed him, very quickly, on the lips. Then she went back inside the apartment and closed the door.

Paolo took the elevator down and went out into the street. People were hurrying under their umbrellas, talking, complaining, laughing. Ordinary people. The extras in the comedy. Paolo watched them and told himself that the scene he had just been through had been simply that—a scene. A brief moment in the comedy, without any particular importance. He told himself that no one had really threatened his life; no one had really warned him that he might be killed. It was impossible that such a thing had really happened.

And yet it had. Just now. An apparently sane girl had told him that he would be killed unless . . . but that was the absurd thing. She hadn't told him the "unless." She had said that her brother wanted to save him. But what did she mean?

Paolo put his umbrella up and started to walk down the street. A mad cripple had seen him at a concert and had fallen in love with him, and now was going to kill him or save him. How obscene it was.

He saw a taxi and hailed it, told the driver his address, got in the back seat, and closed his eyes. He had to do something. But what? He couldn't go to the police, because if he did he would be killed. He wanted to laugh. He imagined telling the story to

Elaine. How she would laugh! Only he wouldn't tell the story to Elaine. He couldn't. Because it wasn't funny, and she couldn't help him. No one could help him except the cripple. . . .

It was unbelievable. A joke, a silly game, he told himself again and again. But he wasn't convinced. He knew that the girl, whether crazy or not, had meant what she said. The girl. Maggie. Maggie and Ralph.

As soon as he was home Paolo looked in the telephone book, found the number of a locksmith, and asked if someone could come immediately and change the lock on his door. He was told a man would be around within the hour.

He wandered around his apartment, and stared at his photographs, his posters, his paintings, his drawings. He imagined the cripple wandering around his apartment, looking at them; touching things, and hopping slowly from room to room. He wanted to throw everything out the window. All his contaminated things. How had the boy—Ralph—how had Ralph got in? When? One of the afternoons he had gone to the beach, perhaps. With some sort of false key. Perhaps Ralph had read his letters. He went to the desk in the living room and opened a drawer. All his letters were there; but they were always in a state of disorder, so it was impossible to tell if someone had been through them. He stirred his hand around in the drawer, and imagined Ralph's hand stirring around, selecting, picking the letters up. He imagined Ralph reading his letters and learning, somehow, the story of his life.

He saw the bright blue envelope with its sheets of bright blue paper inside, and wondered whether Ralph had read that. Christopher's last letter. He turned away from the drawer. That filthy, disgusting letter that Christopher had sent him. He should have thrown it away. But he had kept it, thinking that one day he might be able to show it to Elaine; they might have been able to laugh at it together.

He went over to his armchair and sat down. He had to be logical. Even if Ralph had read his letters, they were not letters by him, but letters to him. They didn't talk about his past. Yet Maggie had seemed to know. He had thought that perhaps she was merely pretending. How could she have learned about him when she had seen him for the first time only two weeks ago? There had been some notes about him on the recital program, but nothing very specific—just about his studies and teachers in Rome, Paris, and Berlin, and the places he had played in. Nothing about his parents, his upbringing, his life. How had she learned so much in so short a time? And how much more did she know? Where had she done her research—or had Ralph done it?

He lit a cigarette, then looked at his piano. He hadn't practiced today. He hadn't practiced for a long time. And on October 26 he had a concert in Palermo. He looked at the calendar. September 25. He had seen the cripple for the first time a week ago, on September 18. Six months to the day after Christopher had died. A week ago, in the newsagent's. The same newsagent's where he had seen Christopher for the first time.

Funny Christopher, with his short legs and long long torso. Christopher with his long freckled face. Christopher, who lisped slightly as he talked; especially when he got excited, which he often did. Christopher talking passionately for hours about politics, about corruption, about famine and poverty; about man-made misery, and the inhumanity of men. Christopher talking so fast he could hardly get his words out. Christopher talking, lisping, denouncing the capitalist system for the havoc it wrought in the minds of men, for the injuries it caused men to inflict upon themselves and others. Rich, rich—as Elaine had said, "rich beyond the dreams of avarice"—Christopher, Christopher getting so excited that tears came into his eyes; and then, suddenly, stopping, and smiling, and saying to Paolo with that smile still on his lips, "Thank God the world is comic, eh, or else it couldn't be borne."

Paolo had said to him once, after he had made one of his speeches, "You're a mess, Christopher." And Christopher had replied, "An ironical mess, I hope?" Paolo had nodded. "I sincerely hope so."

Awkward Christopher, who had become excited only about politics, and music. Christopher, who would fly to Paris for a concert, to Hamburg or London for an opera, and always sit in the very best seats and wear a dark expensive suit—unless he went with Paolo, when he would wear a pair of old jeans and a sweater. But he didn't often go with Paolo, because Paolo didn't like to go with him. Christopher became too excited.

But Christopher had secretly nursed another passion. He had believed in human relationships. He had believed that it was good for human beings to depend on others, rather than on themselves alone. And in that, Paolo thought fiercely, he had been wrong. He had been more than wrong. He had been despicable. He had been weak. He had been wicked.

Paolo saw that he was trembling. He stood up and went over to his desk and put out his cigarette in an ashtray. He looked at his letter drawer; looked at that bright blue envelope. He picked it up. He went back to his chair and sat down again. He took the sheets of paper from the envelope. He looked at the awkward handwriting, the black ink. He imagined Christopher writing it; sitting, wheezing as if he were asthmatic; making that strange noise he always made when he read or wrote anything. He closed his eyes. Christopher. He thought of those talks he had had in those last months of Christopher's life. He remembered Christopher saying, "You know what your trouble is? You've read too much Nietzsche." He remembered how he had snapped back, "Don't be cheap, and cute. I'm talking about something real, something that affects you in this precise moment, something that affects the way you walk and talk and breathe and live."

Oh, no wonder he had never told Elaine about Christopher's return, about those talks they had had. They had been serious. He had felt he was struggling to save Christopher's life. And he had failed. He bit his lips. But his failure had been so unnecessary, so absurd. He *had* saved Christopher's life. He had taken Christopher, when he had returned, hysterical with happiness, from England—and made him see that what he was going to do was wrong. He had convinced him that something so apparently commonplace as a marriage was a compromise which would destroy him. He had convinced Christopher that what was good in him was the contradictions of his own character, and it was only by accepting them, exploring them, becoming aware of their every tiny facet, that he could truly live. He had convinced Christopher that what he thought was love for some girl in England was in fact flight, a petulant reaction to the ending of his friendship with him, Paolo, and Elaine. He had finally convinced Christopher, in those three months—and he had never in his life tried so hard to do anything—that by returning to England, by going ahead with his planned marriage, by believing in the "love" he had for this girl, he was doing something wrong. More than wrong. He was doing something wicked.

But Christopher had been convinced—and there was irony in this, too; fatal irony—only because he was weak. And with his new convictions, and from his weakness, he had written that letter—and Paolo had realized that his apparent success had been, because of Christopher's weakness, the greatest failure of his life.

He opened his eyes and started to read Christopher's letter.

Paolo,

This letter will make you very angry, and I suppose I should know you too well to ask you to forgive me in advance. However, I do, and hope beyond anything that you will—and my hope is to a certain extent justified by the belief that you *want* me to write this.

First, to reassure you. I have not changed my mind. I am not going back to England, and I am not going to get married. I have written—and posted—a definitive letter to that effect this morning.

Anyway . . .

I have asked myself again and again why you are so passionately concerned about my not getting married; about my not returning to England. And you are, have been, concerned; I have never seen you so before. I have been through all the reasons you've given me—your belief in freedom, your belief that I'd be compromising myself, that I was acting out of pique, that I was lying to myself, that I was betraying, if you like, my self and my life—even that I would be doing something falsely "serious." I have been through all these things, all the talks we have had, and yet I still can't understand your concern. All those talks we had were just—talks. I have thought again about everything that happened last year—how you decided we were too close and I was like your brother etc., and how you "dropped" me, and, I

presume, persuaded Elaine to drop me. You know I felt bitter—
we all got on so well together, and your action seemed so point-
less, so childish and spiteful. And then when I had got over feeling
bitter—after all, if you were a rat I should have seen it before (in
fact I did!), but if we had been friendly for all that time I obviously
didn't really care if you were a rat; I even liked you for being a
rat—then, I say, when I was actually happy, when I came back
to Rome to say goodbye forever, you repented of your action.
You wanted me to stay. *Why? Why?* What am I? I have no particular talent in life unless having inherited a lot of money is a
talent. I am intelligent, yes, sure, and can make people laugh if
I want to—but even so—that's not much. It's not even as if our
relationship were physical—if we had been going to bed together
or something that could have been an explanation. But I could,
can, think of no explanation.

This may appear very muddled, and I know I'm telling you
things I've told you a hundred times before, but believe me there
is some sort of logic in what I've written. I can't go through it
because if I do I'll cross everything out and never ever send this,
and I have to. Anyway, Paolo, to come finally to the point. I have
listened to you for the last three months. I have been convinced
by all your talk about freedom and life, etc. But what I want to
say is that though I have nodded and been convinced, every word
you said was crap. C-R-A-P. I didn't, and don't, believe a word of
it, and don't believe you do either. Maybe you do. In any case it's
not important. I let myself be convinced by one thing only, Paolo.
And that is—that I love you. I love you, Paolo. That's all. That's
why I'm staying, and for no other reason. You can interpret that
word love exactly as you please. You can think of it as something
spiritual, physical, or metaphysical. It makes no difference. And
what's more you know it already, even if you pretend not to. That
was why you dropped me last year. You felt it. You even wanted
it perhaps. And now—now you have stopped fighting it. In these
last three months you have accepted it. I don't know what it
means, or implies, or entails for the future. Probably we will just
go on being "friends" for the rest of our lives, with nothing more
between us than the occasional telephone call, dinner together.
I fought against saying the word to myself for a long time, but

—what the hell. You say, and perhaps you believe, that we should live as fully and completely as possible. And it seems to me by admitting this to myself, by actually saying the word "love," I am only doing what you believe or say I should do.

There! The next move, I suppose, is up to you. I would prefer if you wrote me in answer to this, though I presume you'll do what you like. But if you telephone, please call early in the morning, since now that I've decided I'm staying I'm going to get busy and be serious about really settling here. I'm going to go to a lawyer and start doing something about getting a residency permit. Then I shall probably try and buy an apartment—it seems ridiculous paying out all this rent every month—and I must arrange about having my money transferred and—oh, all sorts of things. I guess I should make a new will, too, while I'm about it. Anyway, I'll start tomorrow.

Looking forward to hearing from you, yours,

Christopher

P.S. There's one more thing I should confess. Do you know that I feel sorry for you? I think that that's probably one of the reasons why I love you.

"I guess I should make a new will, too ..." That had been the most abject, disgusting phrase in the whole abject, disgusting letter. Christopher, frightened of failure, had been offering a sort of bribe; saying, in effect, "You'll never have to worry about money any more, neither while I live nor if I should die." He had prefaced it with a whole lot of nonsense about residency permits and buying apartments. He had tried to be so subtle—and his subtlety had been worse than the most outright vulgar offer.

Paolo remembered having told Christopher once, "I'm convinced that people love money, and are prepared to sacrifice themselves for it, in direct proportion to the degree they hate themselves." Had Christopher forgotten that? Or hadn't he believed him? Or had he hoped that deeply, secretly, he did hate himself? Well, he had learned the truth.

Paolo put the sheets of blue paper back in the envelope and held it. He thought of the postcard—it had been the reproduction of a Modigliani nude—he had sent in reply to Christopher's letter; the postcard on which he had scrawled, "Am leaving Rome today. Will not be back. P."

After the locksmith had come, and the lock on the door had been changed, Paolo unplugged the telephone from the wall, took two sleeping pills, and went to bed.

Next morning Ralph was waiting as usual in the newsagent's. Paolo wondered how he should act in the presence of his would-be assassin. But as he had no idea he decided to ignore him completely. Ralph didn't try to speak to him.

That afternoon he didn't even look at his piano. If he had found it almost impossible to practice in the last week, now he found it totally impossible even to consider the idea. And he knew why. His fear of Ralph and the agitation Ralph caused in him were unimportant. It was simply that his technical virtuosity was dependent on his refusing to pass through the printed notes into the foreign lands that lay behind them—and now, whenever he even thought about music, he felt himself being flung, helplessly, across those terrifying frontiers. He was lost; he didn't know a word of the language there; and his panic paralyzed his fingers, his brain, his whole body.

Every day was the same from then on. Ralph; the loathsome piano which, the more he tried to ignore it, became a living thing itself—a heavy mocking creature from another planet, squatting in the corner of the living room; and sleeping pills.

Every day Paolo told himself that he was living in some awful nightmare, from which he would soon awake. And every day, when he went exhausted to bed at about ten o'clock, he knew that it wasn't. It was real. Everything was real. Ralph. Ralph his lover. Ralph his murderer. He felt as if he had a disease that had started with an ache which he had been almost able to ignore; now the ache had developed into a life-threatening tumor, and could be ignored no longer.

One afternoon at two o'clock, ten days after Paolo had followed Ralph, and spoken to Maggie, he went out onto his balcony and looked down and nodded at the cripple.

He let himself out of the apartment and walked slowly down the stairs and out into the street. He went up to the boy and, bowing his head, said, "What do you want me to do?"

He conceded defeat. And as he did so he felt a great wave of relief—almost of happiness—pass over him.

4

"Would you like to come to dinner tonight?" Ralph said eagerly. He sounded as if he were trying to assure Paolo that there was nothing to fear; he also sounded as if he were worried in case Paolo should refuse his invitation.

Paolo didn't refuse, of course; he couldn't. But he had been expecting some strange, unnatural demand. Not a mere invitation to dinner. He stared into the boy's eyes for a second, and smiled. "Yes," he said. "What time and where?"

"Oh, our house. At about eight. Eight-thirty. You know. When you're ready."

Paolo smiled again, feeling foolish as he did so. But his knees were weak.

Ralph looked him up and down, as if checking to see that their clothes still matched. Then he bowed his head and gave a little laugh and murmured, "It took you an awful long time." Paolo saw that he was blushing. The back of his neck was red. He waited till the boy had recovered, and then said, "So I'll see you tonight, then. I must go up and practice now."

Ralph nodded, with a little embarrassed grin on his wet lips. "Yes, you better had," he said.

As Paolo turned away, Ralph called after him, "You know, I'm really sorry if I've been disturbing you."

Paolo hesitated before replying. He reminded himself that he was talking to his would-be murderer. He shrugged, and said, "Oh, that's okay."

As he walked up his stairs he realized that, inexplicably, he had meant it.

He managed to play that afternoon. He felt that, having gone downstairs, and received and accepted Ralph's invitation, a part of his brain had been numbed and anesthetized. When he sat at his piano he thought of nothing but the written notes, and so could play them. He thought of nothing; but his body was excited at the prospect of the evening ahead; it felt alive, and well. More alive, and better, than it had for a long time.

At seven o'clock he stopped practicing. He looked at the calendar. October 5. Exactly three weeks until his concert. If he could practice every day now, until then—every day and all day—he would, perhaps, be able to give a reasonable performance.

He took a shower, washed his hair, and put on a white shirt, a light white sweater, and a pair of black trousers. He couldn't remember when he had last prepared himself for anything with such eager anticipation. Not, perhaps, since the first little recital he had given when he had been twelve years old. Paul Levin. Not quite a child prodigy, but a gifted—exceptionally gifted—child. He remembered the satisfaction he had felt when he had finished playing, and had been applauded by the hundred or so people present. The satisfaction he had felt at hearing the acknowledgment of his talent—of his genius, he had thought at the time. Even before that he had exalted in the strength, the pliancy, the skill of his fingers; but after hearing that applause he had realized that he exalted not only in the skill of his fingers, but of his whole self. It was then that he knew that he had to become a pianist—or that he was a pianist, and had to continue being one.

As he grew older he discovered that he was more intelligent, more skilled, more himself than anyone who might listen to him and applaud him. The applause he received after subsequent concerts never satisfied him to the same degree; satisfied him less and less as the years passed. He wasn't playing for an audience, he realized. He was playing for himself. His playing was a part of himself—a part of himself externalized. Therefore if he didn't practice every day, if he was lazy, it didn't matter. He wasn't producing an end product, to be consumed by the public. He was producing himself. Oh, of course, he had to make his music-as-an-end-product and his music-as-himself match fairly closely, in order to be assured of work. But that wasn't difficult, and without the aid of an agent and without spending any time socializing, as others he knew did, he was offered enough work to live on, what with his concerts, and the private lessons he gave, at exorbitant fees, from November through May of every year.

The public could take what he offered, and no more. It was enough. Later— But he had never allowed himself to think of the future. There was always, and only, the invention of the present.

He went by taxi to Via Francesco Crispi.

As he rang the bell of Maggie's and Ralph's apartment he wondered whether he should have bought some flowers. Flowers. Flowers for his murderers.

Maggie opened the door. She smiled at him; she led him into the living room; she poured him a drink. She said, "I really meant to make dinner myself, here, but I didn't have time to do any shopping." She raised her eyebrows, and her jaw slipped to one side as if she were about to say something more. But she simply shrugged her shoulders, and smiled again.

"What've you been doing with yourself these days?" Paolo asked.

"Sightseeing mainly. I've never been to Rome before. So I go out with a guide book every morning. It's the only thing to do. If one doesn't see everything in the first month one's living in a place, one never does. Don't you think?"

"I guess so. Yes."

Maggie rushed on. "Also, I'm just enjoying my freedom. It's so nice not to work."

"Did you work in London?"

"Yes. I told you, didn't I? I was a secretary. For an impresario who arranged concerts and things."

Paolo nodded.

"I really liked it. I met a lot of very nice people. And I always had tickets for concerts and the opera and the ballet, and as music's about the only thing in the world I manage to get excited—" She stopped, and looked embarrassed. Her face and neck reddened.

"And do you think you're going to like it here?"

Maggie nodded. "Yes, I think I am."

They talked. They chatted. They laughed a bit. They were

polite. But they were a little stiff with each other—like two people who discover that they *do*, after all, have a lot in common, but who, before they can relax with each other, have to forget past and mutual rudeness.

Paolo tried to tell himself that their relationship was as unnatural, dark, and frightening as any that could be imagined. But he couldn't help behaving as if their meeting was that of two civilized people. Two people in a comedy. And he was sure that Maggie felt the same.

They talked for half an hour, and in all this time there was no sign of Ralph. Paolo wondered whether he should ask about him, say his name; he wondered if he would sound forced or awkward if he did.

He tried. "Where's Ralph?"

It came out as easily as if he had been inquiring about Maggie's absent husband, or an old friend.

Maggie frowned. "He's gone out somewhere."

"Ah," Paolo said weakly.

"He's so tiresome. It's his fault we're not eating in tonight. After he'd invited you he didn't telephone me or anything to let me know. He took himself off to a movie, and only came in at about seven. Then he just said vaguely, 'Oh, Paolo's coming to dinner.'" She smiled, apologetically. "And if I cook I like to take a long time about it and there wasn't anything in the house so I thought it would be easier if we went to a restaurant. Are you hungry?"

"Yes. Quite."

"Shall we go, then? Or would you like another drink?"

"What about Ralph? Aren't we going to wait for him? Or is he going to join us somewhere?"

Maggie stood up and frowned again. "Oh, he's not coming. Didn't he tell you?"

"No—I mean—no." Paolo was confused.

"Oh, really he's too much sometimes. I'm sorry."

"Why? I mean—no, perhaps he did say something. Maybe I misunderstood."

"I doubt it. He doesn't explain himself very well. Anyway, I'm afraid it's just me for dinner."

Paolo wondered whether it would be polite to say that he was glad. Then he wondered if he was glad. He said nothing.

"I'll go and fetch my bag. I won't be a second."

They walked to a quiet, expensive restaurant.

While they were eating Paolo said, "What did Ralph do in London?"

"Well, he was at school, of course, until he was sixteen. But then he stopped. There wasn't much point in his going on. He wasn't—he isn't"—she corrected herself gravely—"very bright, and he wasn't learning anything. So it was useless. After that —well, I told you our father went back to America when I was nineteen, and I had a flat. Ralph came to live with me. Daddy didn't want him, so it was the only thing he could do. He used to stay home all day reading—Dickens mainly—and then come to concerts with me in the evening. We used to go to Scotland together in the summer when I had my vacations. That's all. He never did anything, I guess you'd say. Oh, he had a scrapbook that he used to spend hours with everyday, too. He used to collect photographs of murderers and criminals, and reports of crimes, from all the newspapers and magazines." She said it without any special inflection in her voice. Then she looked down at her hands; they were big, and pale, the fingers long and square-tipped, and the nails short and unpainted. She went on, softly, "I didn't want him to work. He's had to suffer enough in his life. And he would only have been hurt by people, I'm sure. And I was making enough for the two of us to live on, just. The flat was cheap—it was in Lambeth—and we never did anything extravagant." She shrugged. "We couldn't. But"—she paused, frowned, and looked up at Paolo—"but it was best like that. Ralph really isn't very well."

"So it was just Dickens."

"And murderers."

"Were you happy?"

Maggie shrugged again.

Paolo suddenly felt very sad. He wanted to touch one of the girl's big pale hands that were lying, still, on the table.

"Do you know London?" she said.

"No, I've never been there."

"Ah."

They ate in silence for a while; then Paolo said, "What about your mother?"

"She and Daddy split up soon after Ralph was born. She went off with some restaurant owner from New York. Ralph would have it that he was a Mafioso and murdered her horribly soon after. I'm sure he wasn't, and didn't, but we always talk about her as if she were dead. I mean, we never talk about her, but—you know. She never tried or wanted to see us after she left Daddy. Or perhaps she did and Daddy told us she didn't so we'd hate her. Anyway. . . ."

When they had finished Maggie called the waiter and asked for the bill. Paolo took his wallet from his pocket, but Maggie said, "Oh, no. I invited you." She put her handbag on the table and opened it and started counting out money, looking proud and childlike as she did. It was a crocodile bag. Maggie left it on the table and gazed defiantly at the waiter as he came to collect the money, as if wanting him to take note that it was she who had paid.

She nodded at the bag. "I'm still not used to all this," she said to Paolo.

"I noticed." He smiled gently at her.

"Oh, dear. I guess I shouldn't make it obvious. Next time you must tell me if I'm behaving badly."

Paolo took one of her hands and squeezed it. "You're not."

She looked at him sharply, as if trying to see in his face the meaning of his gesture. Then she lowered her head and said, "I guess we're going to be awkward with each other for a while."

They took a taxi back to her apartment. Maggie paid for it—again with a slight air of defiance. Paolo had the impression that he couldn't ask where her wealth had come from, apparently so recently. He thought that she would tell him if she wanted to, and for the moment she didn't want to.

They stood on the sidewalk and Maggie said, "Are you going to come up for a drink?"

Paolo hesitated. He wondered what degree of freedom he was allowed, if any. He said, "No, I won't tonight. I'm sort of tired. And I have a lot of practicing to do in the next few days."

Maggie looked disappointed. But she said only, "Oh, yes, of course. When did you say your concert is?"

"The twenty-sixth."

They were both silent, until Paolo said quickly, "You and Ralph will come, won't you?" He wondered, immediately, why he had said it. Perhaps he was hoping to appease any anger that Maggie might feel at his refusal to go upstairs with her.

"Do you *want* us to?"

"Yes. I'd like you to." He said it simply; and as he did he realized that, as when he had said to Ralph that afternoon, "That's okay," he had spoken the truth.

Maggie smiled. "I thought you didn't like friends or family at your concerts."

"How did you know that?"

"I—" Maggie looked embarrassed, and Paolo was certain that she was blushing again, though she was standing in a shadow and he couldn't see. "You told me, didn't you?"

"Oh, yes. You're right," Paolo said. But she wasn't. He hadn't told that to her. He had told many people, but not her. The last person he had said it to had been his mother, the morning he had seen Ralph for the first time. He felt angry for a moment. It wasn't possible that Ralph knew even what he said on the phone. Yet Maggie had quoted him. His exact words. His anger changed to a feeling of sickness; almost despair. He was in the power of monsters.

Maggie was watching him from the shadows. She said, "But we will see each other before then, won't we?" She sounded worried.

He couldn't escape. He had spent a pleasant evening. But it had been a pleasantness permitted him, meagerly portioned out to him, by the rulers of the earth. He was no longer free. And he must not forget it.

"Sure," he said. "When are you free?"

"Oh, I'm always free. When are *you* free?"

"I'm—" he hesitated. "I'm pretty near always free too."

"What about your friends?"

"I never let my friends pin me down."

"Your poor friends." She said it sarcastically—but at the same time, sadly. "Well, if we're both free—how about the day after tomorrow?"

"Yes. Fine. In the evening, though. I must practice in the day."

"Of course. So—say eight o'clock. Thursday evening?"

"Perfect." Paolo stepped forward into the shadows, and without knowing why—but knowing that he wanted to—kissed Maggie on the lips. She put up a hand and held him to her for a moment; then she released him, and whispered, "Thank you."

When Paolo went to the newsagent's the next morning there was no sign of Ralph.

He practiced all day, until eight o'clock, and then went out to dinner with some friends.

He practiced all the day after, too, and in the evening went to meet Maggie. This time he was not excited by the prospect of the evening ahead; nor was he unwilling to spend the evening with the girl. He was obliged to; but the obligation was not onerous.

They ate in. Maggie cooked well. Ralph was not there. He had gone, Maggie said, to a concert. They were shy with each other at the beginning of the evening; shyer than they had been the two other times they had met. But by the time they had finished eating, and had drunk a lot of wine, they had relaxed, and talked to each other freely.

After dinner they sat on a sofa together. Maggie took one of Paolo's hands, and held it. She looked as if she wanted to say something important; but when she did speak it was only, "Would you like to see Ralph's room?"

"Yes. Sure." Paolo stood up. "Is there something special about Ralph's room I ought to see?"

Maggie didn't reply. She led him through the door at the far end of the living room, down a corridor, past the kitchen and a bathroom, and opened a door. She turned on a light, and Paolo stepped forward into Ralph's bedroom. Maggie was watching him, and he tried to keep his face expressionless. But it was difficult. Because on the walls of the room there were giant framed photographs of Ralph. Ralph in the city. Ralph in the country. Ralph in blue jeans. Ralph in a heavy sweater. Ralph in bathing shorts. Ralph nude.

Paolo walked into the center of the room, so that Maggie was behind him. He said, "Where did he have all these taken?"

"Oh, in England."

He turned, and gazed at her. But she was giving nothing away. As if she didn't know about *his* bedroom, *his* photographs.

"It's rather—bizarre," he said.

"I don't know if it's that." Maggie gave a crooked smile. "I think it's grotesque. Especially that one." She pointed at Ralph in his bathing shorts. "That awful would-be sexy pose." She said, very quietly, "Poor baby."

Paolo looked around the room again. At the photographs. At the big unmade bed. At the white and gold wardrobe. At the chest of drawers. At the gray and gold bedside table. He stared at the bedside table. On it there was a gold lamp with a parchment shade; a paperback edition of *Bleak House*—and a gun, two knives, and two pairs of handcuffs.

Maggie whispered, "It's horrible, isn't it? I get so frightened by them."

Paolo walked over to the table and looked down. One of the knives—its blade must have been twelve inches long—was rusty. As if it had been used. As if there were blood on it, that had dried.

"Please don't touch anything. He always keeps that gun loaded and cocked."

Paolo looked at the gun. It was small, and black, and just like the one that the police had shown him in Christopher's apartment; the gun that killed Christopher.

Maggie said, "I never come in here. I make Ralph tidy up. I can't bear it."

And yet she didn't mind that Ralph had sentenced him to death. She didn't mind that Ralph was prepared to use one of these weapons on him. Not only did she not mind; she approved.

"And you brought all this from London with you?"

"Yes. We came by train. I was terrified that our bags would be searched by the customs. But Ralph said they would never search him."

"They never search anyone on trains."

"I didn't know. I told you, I've never been on the Continent before. Just America and England." She added, "I did make him unload the gun, though, while we were traveling." She turned out the light and left the room, and Paolo followed her. "It was the first thing he did when we arrived. Reloaded it."

They stood in the corridor, and Paolo looked down at the floor. "Don't you mind?" he said.

"Mind?" For a moment, obviously, she didn't know what he meant. Then she seemed to understand him—from his tone, perhaps, more than his words. "You mean Ralph and I—together?"

Paolo nodded.

"Yes. In a way, of course I do. I mean, I'm a very ordinary girl and I'd quite like to lead an ordinary life. But I did, more or less, until last year. Then last year everything seemed to get out of control." She took his hand, and led him down the corridor, and opened the door of the room next to Ralph's. She didn't turn on the light.

She led him across the room to her bed, and got on it, and lay down. "Lie down beside me please," she whispered, but it was an order. Paolo told himself that he should rebel; but he didn't. He tried to tell himself that it was because he couldn't; but then he admitted that it was because he didn't want to. He *wanted* to lie down next to Maggie. Next to Ralph's sister. . . .

He got onto the bed.

"I was quite happy until last year," Maggie said. "I never thought about the future—or if I did I thought that I'd go on working, and looking after Ralph, and that we'd have our own sort of life together. I do love him, you see. And I know you think that everyone should go through life free and independent and everything, but I honestly can't think what for. I have nothing particular to give—either to myself or to other people. Only to Ralph. I can—or could—give something to him. And we were happy with each other. I can't say any more. That's my justification for our life together, if any justification's needed. And I don't think it is," she said fiercely, in the darkness.

"Anyway, everything was fine until July of last year. Then one evening Ralph came home and told me that he was in love. I guess you would have laughed, and I might have too. But I didn't. I just felt terribly hurt when he said it. I immediately had visions of Ralph—I don't know—I suppose he couldn't have gone off and left me, but I didn't think. I just felt that there was I who had, for the last four years at least, devoted my life more or less exclusively to him—and now, suddenly, *he* was in love. He was going to give *me* up. It wasn't fair. I guess I'd always thought that it was I who was sacrificing any chance of leading a really ordinary life— getting married maybe, having children—or even getting a good job that involved socializing or something out of office hours. But then I realized that Ralph thought I was only looking after him for my own satisfaction. Well, maybe I was. I mean—I'm not explaining myself very well. Anyway when he told me that he had fallen in love I was very hurt, and burst into tears. It was ridiculous. Ralph just watched me. He didn't say a word or try to comfort me. Eventually I pulled myself together and asked him who with. 'A man,' he said. And then I'm afraid I did laugh, and that was even worse than crying. But it was all such a shock. But I only laughed for a second, and then I asked him if this man was in love with him. Then I was ashamed of myself. I sounded so bitchy. But Ralph came over to me and took my hand and said, 'No, of course not. He doesn't even know. But I am in love with him and I'm going to have him, for you.'

"Then he explained what he meant. He was going to introduce me to this man. He'd met him at a concert that I hadn't gone to for some reason the night before and they'd sat next to each other and started talking. The man had mentioned he was going to another concert the week after—so Ralph said we'd have to go. That way we could meet him. The idea was that I was to meet him, and fall in love with him. And he was to meet me and fall in love with me. And that way Ralph could have him, vicariously. Through me, as it were. When Ralph explained all this to me I was really touched, and upset that I'd been so nasty and selfish to him when he told me. Because it was all so absurd and ridiculous. The whole idea.

"Anyway, I started crying again, and put my arms around Ralph and told him that I loved him more than I could ever love anyone else and that he was so sweet to have thought of this crazy scheme—and I asked him what was in it for him. Apart from the vicarious thrill. And he said that I mustn't worry about him, that he would be able to take care of himself. That I mustn't think he would want to come and live with me and my husband when we were married. I told him that I would never marry anyone if it meant giving him up. Then he got really angry with me. He said that if I did fall in love with this unknown man, and this unknown man fell in love with me—if I tried to refuse him on the grounds that I couldn't leave him—Ralph, I mean—he would kill himself. And he meant it. So he told me that I had to promise him, swear to him, that if what he had planned did happen, I *would* get married, and not take him into consideration. He said the day I got married would be the greatest, happiest day of his life, and I had no right to deprive him of such happiness."

Maggie sighed. "I promised him. And absurd or ridiculous or not, it happened. I met this man at the concert. He was very nice. But remembering what Ralph had said, I didn't want to see him again, though he asked me out to dinner. I said no. Ralph was furious with me. He wouldn't speak to me for five days. But somehow or other he engineered another meeting. I guess he telephoned the man—we knew his name, and Ralph must have looked him up in the telephone book or something—and told him that I'd only refused to go out with him because I was afraid of falling in love with him because I didn't want to leave Ralph. We met 'by chance' in a restaurant. And after that everything became a sort of beautiful nightmare. We went out together alone, and went away for the weekend together—without Ralph. We slept together. And after about three months he asked me to marry him. I didn't know what to do. The whole affair had some terrible, awful logic about it. I knew if I refused Ralph would know immediately—the man would have told him. They were friendly. Already like brothers-in-law. Besides, I had promised Ralph I would marry him if I loved him. And I did love him. He was kind and wonderful and offered me—well, let's say happiness. Maybe even if I hadn't promised Ralph I would have accepted. In any case, I did. We were going to get married.

"For a month everything was perfect. I'd never been so happy, and I'd never seen Ralph so happy. And then—it was over. He went away, and didn't come back. He wrote, of course, and said he was coming. But as time went by I knew it wasn't true. I thought that perhaps he had realized that by marrying me he'd also be marrying Ralph, even though Ralph had already arranged to stay on in my flat, and we were going to get a house in Hempstead. I would have given Ralph money every week, of course, but— Then, when he didn't come back and didn't come back, and his letters arrived, and then stopped arriving, I stopped thinking that. I stopped thinking anything. And then the last, final letter arrived. I've never been so miserable in my life. Ralph's whole mad plan. It had worked so perfectly. Until, suddenly—pouf. It was so terrible. As if the world had changed its course. Ralph had planned something and mad though it was there was logic in it. And then logic seemed to have failed. And—oh, God."

Paolo felt Maggie shaking on the bed beside him. He took one of her hands and squeezed it. She started talking again. "Ralph started disappearing for days at a time. Once he was gone for ten days. I didn't know where he went. I didn't care. I didn't ask him. I was too miserable. I went to the office and came home and didn't know what I was doing. Then, after a couple of months, I started to pull myself together. I told myself what the hell, there'd be someone else. I didn't believe it, of course, at the beginning. But as time passed, and for force of telling myself, I started to realize that it was true. I was just going through what everyone who had had an unhappy love affair went through—everyone, anyone who's been abandoned by the person they love. I told myself it was just as well he had left me—if he was the sort of person who could act as he had acted, then he wasn't worth having anyway. Of course, that wasn't true, either, because I knew what his character was like, and I knew that he was someone who always wanted to act in good faith, who was terrified of betraying his integrity, and because of that might have done something that seemed to him to be right, but was really weak and wrong. I would have forgiven him anything.

"Then one day at the beginning of this last June—four months ago—I got home from the office and found Ralph waiting for me. He was holding a letter in his hands. But before he gave me the letter he told me that the man I had been going to marry was dead. I just stared at him, and thought I would faint. Because with all those knives, and that gun, and his scrapbook full of murders, and his disappearances—I was sure, I was absolutely convinced that Ralph had murdered my fiancé. And I just didn't dare ask him about it, or say anything. My only thought was that *he* was dead, and—I just sat down on the floor. I was too stunned to cry or do anything. I didn't know what to do. I just sat there and stared.

"And then Ralph gave me the letter he'd been holding. I opened it and read it as if it were written in a foreign language. But when I had finished I understood, and it seemed to be the ultimate ironical twist of the knife. The letter was from a solicitor. I had been left a lot of money. A really enormous amount of money. And so on the same day I had been condemned and given the means of release.

"I guess I acted insanely after that. Next morning I went to my bank—I had about two hundred pounds saved up in case of emergencies—and took all that money out. I bought Ralph a plane ticket, and put him on a plane to Paris. I told him to stay there in some small hotel and wait until I could join him, or at least decide what to do. He went, and phoned me that night to tell me where he was staying.

"I told the office I was sick, and stayed home and cried for two days. Then I went to see the solicitor who had written me. After that I tried to call Ralph in Paris. But he had checked out of the hotel, and they didn't know where he had gone. I was frantic, but there was nothing I could do. I stayed in London. I quit my job. Then one day toward the end of August, Ralph turned up. He looked quite well and calm. He told me he had changed hotels in Paris because he'd wanted to be completely alone, and cut off, so he could think. He was sorry if he had worried me. Then he said he had decided we should leave London and go and live in Italy for a while. I didn't care, so I said okay. Ralph said I should leave all the arrangements up to him. I gave him some money—the lawyer had given me an advance until all the money that had been left me came through, and everything was settled legally. Ralph bought tickets, made reservations, and planned our itinerary. We left London on the afternoon of September twelfth by train.

Next morning we arrived in Milan. That evening we went to your concert."

Paolo's eyes had become accustomed to the dark; he could see a lamp on a table by the bed. He turned it on and propped himself up on his elbows and looked down into Maggie's face. He looked down at the pale skin, at the brown curly hair, at the dark eyes, at the wide mouth.

"I've told you everything I'm going to tell you," Maggie said softly. "And you mustn't ask any questions. I'll tell you the rest some other time. Okay?"

Paolo whispered, "Okay." But he hadn't been going to ask her any questions. He didn't want to know any more, now, or ever. He didn't even want to know as much as she had told him.

He lowered his head toward her. Toward Maggie's face. Toward Ralph's face. . . .

"Close your eyes," Maggie whispered.

He closed his eyes, but still he saw Ralph's face. He stretched out a hand and turned off the light. Then, not knowing whether he had lowered his head further, or whether Maggie had raised hers, he was kissing her.

They started to make love.

Paolo practiced the next day until eight, then went to meet Maggie. They ate, they talked, and they made love. He had never, in his life, found such satisfaction in sex.

The day after was spent in the same way, and the day after, and the day after that.

Paolo never saw Ralph.

One evening Paolo took Maggie to a restaurant where he had often eaten with Elaine. When they arrived, Elaine was sitting, lank-haired, tiny, and alone at a table in the corner.

Paolo introduced Maggie to her. Elaine shook hands with the girl and said to Paolo, "Well, I'm glad your problems are over. No more cripples, eh?"

Paolo was furious, Maggie looked embarrassed, and Elaine was drunk. Paolo said, "I'll call you soon," and Elaine said in a false, exaggerated British accent, "That's awfully good of you, old chap."

Paolo, at their table, told Maggie about Elaine, about Elaine's marriage, and about their friendship. When he had finished Maggie said, "That's sort of sad."

"Why?"

"Well, she doesn't look as though she sees the comedy of the situation, in your abandoning her"—she hesitated—"for me."

Paolo didn't, either. "But we were never lovers, or anything like that," he said.

"That makes it even sadder. Don't you think you have a duty to your friends?"

"I haven't really had time for my friends recently." Paolo smiled. "And it hasn't been entirely my fault."

"Oh, I know," Maggie said seriously. "But I was thinking that perhaps you could introduce me to some of your friends. We could all go out together some evening. But I guess Elaine wasn't too happy about being introduced to me."

"My other friends would be. And she'll get over it. If she doesn't, then—hard luck for her."

"Yes," Maggie said doubtfully. Then she looked up at Paolo and asked, half humorously, "*We're* not friends, are we?"

Paolo avoided her eyes. "No," he said. "I guess we're not."

After a while Maggie said, "Anyway, even if she doesn't behave with the perfect tact that a friend of yours is supposed to possess, I feel sort of sorry for her."

"You shouldn't."

"Oh, I know."

"You shouldn't feel sorry for anyone."

"I know that too. But I do, for quite a lot of people. I don't for Ralph, at all." She put her fork down and said gently, "But I do for you."

Paolo drew back in his chair. He felt disgusted with Maggie, disgusted with himself, disgusted with his whole situation. It was insane. He said, trying to keep his voice down, "And why do you feel sorry for me?"

Maggie glanced at him, surprised, and smiled. "Oh, dear. I've offended you. You shouldn't be offended. I'm probably wrong, and stupid. It's just that you do take yourself terribly seriously, Paolo. And then—you know, the first time I ever saw you, at your concert, I felt sorry for you. But"—she paused, and appeared to change her mind about what she was going to say—"just at this particular moment, Ralph and I have put you into the most intolerable situation, haven't we?" She raised her eyebrows, smiled, and waited to see how he would take it.

Paolo bit his lower lip. He said, "I thought exactly that not ten seconds ago." He looked at her and smiled. But he wished he could leave Maggie and go over to Elaine, sitting in the corner, and start talking and laughing with her.

Maggie lowered her eyes. "But you know, if I didn't feel sorry for you I wouldn't be here now. You'd be unbearable. And unbelievable."

Paolo studied the plates on the table. The knives and the forks. The pepper mill. The glass containers of oil and vinegar. Frightened, somehow, that Elaine would hear him speak, he murmured, "Maggie, this isn't all some sick joke you're playing on me?"

Maggie shook her head. "No," she said. "I'm sorry. It isn't." She, too, was speaking to the table. "If it was just up to me things would never have got to this point. I mean none of this would have happened. But it isn't up to me. It's Ralph. And please"—she looked up at him, and her voice was urgent—"*please* don't think it's a joke. Because it isn't. Ralph will kill you if—"

"If what? If he can't 'save' me?"

Maggie nodded.

"But what does he want? What does he mean?" Paolo sighed. "*How* is he going to save me, Maggie?"

"Didn't you understand the other evening when I told you that long story about what happened in London?"

"I don't understand anything."

"Oh, Paolo." Maggie sounded irritated. "Don't you see? You *must* see. You've got to marry me."

Paolo didn't know what to do or where to look. He turned in his chair and stared toward Elaine. She was smiling at him.

5

Paolo looked away from Elaine and back at Maggie. But she avoided his eyes.

He couldn't speak to her here. Not with Elaine sitting over there, smiling.

They ate steaks and salads in silence, and as soon as they had finished Paolo asked for the bill, without asking Maggie whether she wanted any fruit or cheese. He couldn't say a word to her.

Maggie made no attempt to pay, and as soon as the waiter brought Paolo his change they stood up, turned together toward Elaine and nodded at her, as if they had been rehearsed in their movements. From her corner Elaine raised a hand, almost waving at them. Then she dropped the hand onto the table and looked at it, as if she couldn't remember why she had raised it.

They left the restaurant. Paolo took Maggie's arm. They were going to walk home. They had to talk.

Paolo started. He spoke slowly, distinctly and, he hoped, reasonably. He said, "Maggie, I like you, and under the circumstances we get on quite well together. But you're intelligent. You must see that this whole business is completely mad."

They walked on for some time before Maggie replied. "Yes. I guess it is."

"Well, then?"

"But it doesn't make any difference."

"But—" Paolo sighed. "Maggie, I'm not going to marry you. I'm not going to marry anyone, ever. And *you* can't marry me because Ralph tells you you've got to. You don't even know me."

"I trust Ralph," Maggie said softly.

"What does that mean?"

"It means that Ralph is in love with you and thinks that you're" —she smiled—"worthy of me. I suppose that sounds awful, but what I mean is that I do want to marry you. I want to have a relationship with you, and I'm prepared to commit myself to that relationship, and I want you to commit yourself to it."

"And what is Ralph proposing to do? If we get married he'll come and live with us and the first time we have a fight he'll blow my brains out."

"I don't know what Ralph's going to do. We haven't discussed it. All I know is that Ralph loves you, and thinks that I will. He was right before, and he'll probably be right now."

"But he *wasn't* right before."

"In a way. But that was because things got out of control. This time he's not going to let them."

They could have been talking about some unimportant business transaction; not a matter of life and possibly death, Paolo thought.

"And his idea is that if I marry you I'll be saved, and if I don't —or if I do, and leave you—I'll be killed?"

"I don't know."

Paolo looked at the tall girl with a crooked jaw, dressed in black, holding his arm, and staring gravely at the sidewalk in front of her.

They stopped; but Maggie continued to stare at the sidewalk.

"Maggie," Paolo said, "do you really want to marry me?"

She turned slowly to him and looked at his face for a while before saying seriously, "Yes, Paolo, I do."

"But *why?*"

"Because I'll love you."

Paolo dropped her arm.

"And also"—she smiled, sadly—"this will probably make you angry, but while we're talking—I think if we got married I could help you. Or, if you like it better, save you."

Paolo shook his head; he couldn't speak.

"You see, I said back there in the restaurant that I felt sorry for you the first time I saw you. And it's true. Because I was sitting listening to you and you made me feel sad for some reason. You were playing beautifully, but"—she paused, searching for words —"you'll probably think I'm a fool if I say this, but when you were playing I couldn't help feeling that you didn't know *what* you were playing. I got the impression that you were completely lost. As if you were in a foreign country and didn't know the language."

Paolo stared at her. He felt hopeless. She knew what his apart-

ment was like. She knew about his past. And now ... she was a
witch.

But Maggie was still talking; faster now. "You'll tell me I got
that impression because I wanted to, because my reaction was
subjective. But I'm sure it wasn't only that. It made me terribly
nervous listening to you, because I *knew* when you were going
to make actual technical mistakes. All the time you were right
on the edge of that foreign country, but occasionally I could feel
you slipping over the border, as it were. And when you did, sure
enough, you made a mistake. But I could tell from the reactions
of the other people there—from the way they moved, or listened,
or breathed while you were playing—that most of them thought
you were playing with great sensitivity. But you weren't. It was
just your lostness that gave that impression. And it's not the same
thing at all. Am I a fool?"

Paolo took her arm, and they walked on down the road. He
cleared his throat before he said, "No, and yes."

"Fifty-fifty?"

"No. A hundred a hundred."

"Ah."

They walked on.

"I'm not a fool," Maggie said, "for having said what I said, but
I'm a fool for thinking I could do anything about it?"

"Yes. Look, Maggie. I don't want any help. I'm happy as I am. I
like to play the piano—to be a pianist—just because of the technical element. I love to be able to control myself to that extent. And
I don't always make mistakes. Sometimes I can play for a whole
evening and not make a single mistake. Then I *am* brilliant. And
it's just me. I don't have to turn to anyone—not the composer, or
the public, or anyone—to borrow anything. I don't have to use
sentiment or secondhand feelings to get my effect." He smiled
at her. "I'm just great. Sometimes. That's what I try for, anyway.
And I don't need anyone's help."

Maggie said earnestly, "But are you great by your own definition, or are you what the world calls great?"

"I don't give a fuck for the world."

"You live in it."

"Maggie, I'm not going to marry you, and you're just going to

have to persuade your dear brother not to kill me. Tell him you'd
be harming my music instead of helping it."

"It wouldn't do any good."

Paolo suddenly laughed. "Oh, Jesus, isn't this all *ludicrous!*"

"Yes," Maggie said, without feeling.

They didn't speak again until they stood in the street outside
Maggie's apartment.

"I don't think I'll come up," Paolo said.

"Please do. I want you to."

Paolo hesitated.

"You must come up," Maggie said.

After they had made love Maggie said, "I want you to sleep
here tonight."

Paolo didn't reply. He lay on his back with his eyes closed.

Maggie sounded amused. "Paolo, do you really think that
you're so great, or is it that the world's so awful?"

Paolo pretended he was falling asleep.

Maggie said, "Have you ever been in love?"

"No. Never."

It wasn't true. But he wasn't going to tell her about it. He had
only ever told three people about it—two of whom were Elaine
and Christopher—and he had forbidden them to draw any conclusions from his story. But he knew that Maggie would draw
conclusions, so he decided not to tell her anything. She would
think that what had happened provided some sort of psychological explanation—or, worse, excuse—for the way he thought and
acted and lived. She would think that his life-style had been forced
on him by a psychological trauma, whereas it was in fact the
coolly considered result of a moral decision he had made when
he was—how old? He wondered. Fourteen, when he had left
America? Twelve, when he had given his first concert? Earlier?
He didn't know. It didn't matter when first he had made it. What
mattered was that he had made it, and made it anew, every day,
every moment. Having been in love was nothing to do with the
way he lived. How cheap psychology was. . . .

He lay in the darkness, and thought about that time in Paris.

He had been nineteen. He was studying in Paris for a year.

He had met a girl at the Conservatoire; a blonde half-Russian, half-French girl. Twenty-three, and also a pianist; she was small, and looked Russian, and everything about her was fine. Her face, her bones, the way she moved, the way she talked. Her mind was fine, and her playing was fine; too fine. It was perfect, and precise; but she approached her music as if she were on equal terms with it, instead of being its master. She knew this, and didn't care. She laughed a lot, and could tell jokes and discuss literature in six different languages. She said she was a Catholic, but loathed the idea of religion.

She and Paolo liked each other. After they had known each other for three days they started sleeping together, some nights in her large apartment, some nights in Paolo's tiny apartment. They liked each other; there was nothing more to the affair. They continued sleeping together for three months—generally four nights out of seven. Then one afternoon Natasha—her name was Simone, but Paolo had always called her Natasha and she had laughingly gone along with it—told Paolo that she had fallen in love and wanted him, as a friend whose judgment she could trust, to meet Jean-Louis, and tell her what he thought.

That evening they all went out to dinner; Natasha introduced Paolo to Jean-Louis as a friend she had known all her life. When they were together Paolo called her Simone, and he called Jean-Louis Jean-Louis , though he thought of him as simply Jean. Jean was a thief. He was charming, handsome, vulgar, and Corsican. He worked for—or, as far as Paolo could tell, was the head of —a ring of art thieves who stole old masters on commission for wealthy Americans, South Americans, and Japanese. Natasha was obviously fascinated by him, and hardly took her eyes off him the whole evening; he treated her with such gentleness and tenderness that she might have been the most fragile, priceless painting that he had ever removed from the wall of a house that was wired for thieves. He treated Paolo as if he were a light that shone on the beautiful painting; with a mixture of courtesy, respect, gratitude, and total disregard.

They ate—of course, Paolo thought—at Maxim's, and by the end of the evening he was intoxicated by the drink, the situation, by Natasha, and by Jean.

Or rather, he told himself when he lay alone in bed at the end of the evening, he was intoxicated by Natasha *and* Jean. He tried to sleep; he couldn't. He tried to think of the next day; he couldn't. He could think of nothing but Natasha and Jean, and he realized that he was in love with them. Not with Natasha alone; she was beautiful and fine, and she was a friend. Nor with Jean alone; he was exotic, strangely old-fashioned, probably dangerous, and had nothing in common with a nineteen-year-old pianist. But together . . . he was in love with them. He wanted to be with them.

He supposed what he felt was unusual; but what did that matter? He was an unusual person—and besides, there were no rules as to whom one could or could not fall in love with.

He saw a lot of them in the following weeks; they both liked to have him about. But if one day Natasha didn't call, he became so agitated that he couldn't eat, couldn't play the piano, couldn't do anything except think of *them*. He always managed to hide his feelings from them. He was, simply, a friend. Cheerful, witty, talented. If he was sometimes depressed, it never occurred to them that they might be the cause of his depression. And if they did comment on his being low occasionally, he would say it was because he was studying too hard, or because he had a hangover, or because of the weather.

Then, after this had been going on for almost three months, Natasha didn't call him for two days. Then three days. He became frantic. He felt sick. On the fourth day, when there was still no call, he had to force himself not to go to Natasha's apartment. On the fifth day he stayed in bed. On the evening of the sixth day Natasha called and whisperingly, laughingly, apologized for her silence. Jean, she said, had been doing "a job," and she had been so nervous she hadn't felt capable of speaking to anyone. But the job had been successful. Could they all have dinner together tonight? They would go to Maxim's again, to celebrate. Paolo said he couldn't. Natasha, sounding worried, asked him if he was sick. He said no, but she heard something strange in his voice, and said she would come over immediately to see how he was. He told her not to. But he didn't sound convincing; he couldn't.

Natasha came. After she had been questioning him for two minutes Paolo started crying. He couldn't stop. He became hysterical. Natasha asked him what was wrong, begged him to tell her. He told her. He saw her fine face flush, as if she had heard something obscene. She said very softly that she was sorry, that she should have realized, that it was all her fault. But Paolo had seen her expression. He didn't say anything. He went on crying, and she wandered around his room looking at her hands. Eventually she said again that she was sorry, but she supposed it was best if they didn't see each other any more.

Paolo chokingly asked her not to tell Jean. She said quickly, gently, that of course she wouldn't; but he guessed that, sooner or later, she would.

She left.

He stayed in his apartment, in bed. He couldn't eat anything. He cried, he shook, he vomited. One morning he felt so sick he called a friend of his and asked him to come over. The friend came, saw him, and called an ambulance. Paolo struggled, fought, and cried as he was carried down the stairs and put into the ambulance. He was taken to a psychiatric hospital. He stayed there a month. He saw a psychiatrist every day and told him the whole story. The psychiatrist was small, pleasant, and stuttered slightly.

At the end of the month he could talk about the affair with sufficient composure to be able to smile about it. He left the hospital and flew back to America to stay with his parents. At the end of the month he was so bored that he thought that madness in Paris was preferable.

Back in Paris, he started to become depressed again, thinking about Natasha and Jean. But gradually he got used to the depression, until, he realized, he had almost forgotten that he was depressed. He was better.

He bumped into Natasha one day in the street—she had stopped frequenting the Conservatoire. Paolo liked to think she had stopped because she didn't want to see him; but she said, standing in the street, that it was because she no longer felt that she *was* a pianist. Later, maybe, she would go back to it, and meanwhile she was practicing every day at home. They said goodbye.

Paolo met her again in the same street four days before he was leaving Paris to go on to Berlin. She said she was pregnant. Jean had given up stealing pictures; he had put the money he had made into some boutiques in Paris and St. Tropez, and into a plant that processed waste plastic or something. She wasn't quite sure what it was. They were going to get married. Paolo wished her luck. Again they said goodbye, and as Paolo walked away from her he realized that he was not so much disappointed in them as disgusted with himself. He had been in love with them. In a month or two, or perhaps a year or two, he would be able to smile at himself, laugh at himself, forgive himself. But in the meantime he was disgusted with himself. He hoped he never would be again.

Some time had passed since he had grunted, "No, never," at Maggie. Now he stopped thinking about the past, and relaxed, shifting slightly in the bed. .... He could feel that Maggie, beside him, was still awake—and as he moved, she moved too. He waited for her to speak, but another five minutes passed before she murmured, "*Never*? Not even when you were younger? Didn't you fall in love then? When you were eighteen or nineteen? Everyone does."

He had forgotten that she was a witch. "What about you?" he said. "Did you fall in love when you were nineteen?"

"Ralph came to live with me when I was nineteen."

"Oh, yes." He stared up into the darkness, and gave a mental shrug. "Yes," he said. "I was in love when I was nineteen."

He told her the story.

When he had finished she laughed. "You're funny."

"Why?"

"Well, you sound so apologetic. As if you were telling me something terribly deep." He heard her smiling in the darkness. "I mean, it makes a good story, and I'm sorry you were in a madhouse for a month, but really—it's no excuse."

"I didn't mean it to be." He sounded petulant.

"No?" Maggie laughed again. "Oh, well. Goodnight. Sleep well."

Paolo woke at nine. Maggie was still asleep. He heard someone moving about the apartment. Ralph. He closed his eyes.

At eleven Maggie shook him. "Come along, wake up. You

must go home and practice. You've got a concert in a week."

"I was awake. I was dreaming."

"Well, get up."

He got up and dressed. Sitting on the edge of the bed, he looked around the room.

"What've you done with my jacket?"

"I don't know. Isn't it here?"

"No."

"You must have thrown it on the chair in the hall when we came in last night. I'll go and look."

She came back almost immediately holding the leather jacket. "It was there."

Paolo took it and felt in his pockets. His wallet. His keys. A pair of dark glasses. They were all there. Perhaps he had taken it off as soon as he'd come in the door last night. But he didn't think so. He was sure he had gone straight to Maggie's bedroom and started to undress there.

"Where's Ralph?"

"I don't know. Why? Are you afraid of meeting him?"

"No, but—"

"Anyway, don't worry. He's either gone out, or he's shut up in his room reading, or looking at his photographs and masturbating." She smiled, and shrugged her shoulders.

"Look, Maggie," Paolo said. "Last night—well—what I mean is—" He stopped. He couldn't say what he wanted to say. Instead he said, "Do you mind if we don't see each other this week, until my concert? I've got to concentrate, and—" He hoped she would understand him.

She looked hurt. "Yes, I mind," she said. "But all right. How are we all going down to Palermo?"

"We'll talk about it on the phone. Okay?"

Maggie turned away and murmured, "Okay."

Paolo walked home. It was a fine sunny morning. He felt curiously at ease. Curiously, because he had decided he wasn't going to see Maggie any more. He believed all that she said; he believed that she meant it when she told him that Ralph would kill him if he didn't marry her. And yet, suddenly, he felt that what was

happening no longer concerned him. As if it wasn't he who was
threatened, but someone called Paolo who had been invented by
the brother and sister. A mere image of Paolo. In any case, he
was going to call their bluff for the moment. He had to. Because
he wasn't going to marry anyone—especially not an intense
and lonely ex-secretary with a crippled brother. He was free. He
looked up at the blue October sky and told himself that he was
free.

When he got home he sat at his piano and played for half an
hour, then went to the window and looked up at the blue sky. He
was free. He felt as if he were doped. He didn't want to practice,
but he had to. He had a concert in a week. He went back to the
piano, played for another half hour, and then stood up and left
the apartment.

He started walking. Slowly. It was a beautiful day. He was free.
Everything else was a dream, and didn't concern him. If Maggie
and Ralph didn't concern him—if his own death didn't concern
him—how could a concert concern him? In a dream, he went up
to the park at Colle Oppio and sat looking at the golden trees and
the children, golden in the autumn light. He was free. He stood
up and started walking again. He went to a restaurant and sat
at a table outside and had lunch. Afterward he started walking
again. Paolo Levin. He considered him. Paolo in photographs.
Paolo on posters. Paolo on paper. Paolo on canvas. No. Not even
that concerned him.

He walked until half past four, and then began to feel cold. He
started toward home; and as he walked he realized that he wasn't
going to give a concert next week. He would send a telegram
saying he was sick three days before. He had a doctor friend
who would give him a certificate if necessary. He would ask if
his concert could be postponed for a month. He had never done
it before, but people he knew had. Just once wouldn't harm his
reputation. He would have to do it. He couldn't give a concert in
Palermo. Not with Ralph and Maggie present. He couldn't give a
concert anywhere.

He lay on his bed and looked at the photographs of himself.

They seemed to be smiling at him. Telling him he had made the right decision. Telling him that he was free, and could do as he pleased. He was in a dream.

The telephone rang. He jumped. He had been asleep. He picked up the receiver and said, "Hello?"

"Paolo, it's me, Maggie."

"Hello, Maggie," he said sleepily.

"Where've you been? I've been trying to reach you all day."

"I went out for a walk. It's so beautiful out." He was smiling. "Listen, Maggie. I've decided I'm not going to Palermo. I'm going to send a telegram saying I'm sick." He felt very happy as he told her; happy, and confidential, like a child who has just learned the facts of life and is telling them to a friend.

"Paolo, are you all right?"

"Yes, I'm fine. Very well."

"You sound strange."

"I fell asleep when I got in."

"Listen, Paolo. I told Ralph that I wouldn't be seeing you for a week, and—I'm sorry, but I've got to see you tonight."

Happily, Paolo said, "I'm afraid that's impossible, Maggie."

"I've *got* to." She sounded worried.

"I tell you, it's impossible."

"Ralph says you've got to come around tonight. He insists."

"Who's Ralph?"

"Paolo, *please.*"

"No. I don't care what Ralph says. I'm free."

"Come for me, then. Please."

"No, Maggie. I don't want to see you tonight."

"Don't you understand me?"

"Yes. Perfectly. It's you who don't seem to understand." He looked at his photographs. They were smiling at him. He said, "Look, I'll call you in a day or two. Look after yourself, and love to Ralph. 'Bye."

He put the phone down, feeling very pleased with himself. He wondered if he should call some friends and see them. Or go to a movie. Or to a concert, if there was one. Or . . . he fell asleep again.

When he woke he was cold. He looked at his clock. It was five o'clock in the morning. He shivered, then pulled off his clothes and crawled under the covers. He was very cold. He closed his eyes and told himself to go back to sleep. But then he remembered the day before; and he was awake. He remembered his decision to cancel his concert. He remembered that he had refused Maggie's invitation—Maggie's order.

Paolo turned on the lamp by his bed and looked at his photographs. They were smiling at him; but in derision. They were mocking him. He had refused Maggie's order. He was not going to give his concert. He shivered. He was cold and frightened. Maggie and Ralph were threatening his career. They were threatening his life. He had to get away from them. But he couldn't. Ralph would follow him. Perhaps he should call Maggie now. Apologize, say he was coming over, say he would marry her . . . No. It was madness. He couldn't. He had to get away. He was trembling uncontrollably. Get away. Where to? Home. Oh, yes. He had to go home.

He had tears in his eyes. He wiped them with the back of his hand, got up, and ran into his bathroom. He was so cold. He had to have a bath. He turned on the hot water and stood by the side of the tub, waiting for it to fill, hearing his teeth chattering, seeing his whole body shaking. He tried to get hold of himself, but he couldn't. His body was out of control. He looked in a mirror, and hardly recognized what he saw there. A strained, frightened, shaking body. A body out of control. His body. Paolo Levin. A ridiculous puppet with chattering teeth. He turned away from the mirror. He had lost himself.

He almost scalded himself in the bath, but within five minutes of getting out he was cold again. He dressed in his warmest clothes, packed a small bag with his washing things and a pair of jeans and a couple of T-shirts and sweaters, and ran out of the apartment.

He ran most of the way to the station, looking over his shoulder occasionally, to see if anyone was following him. But he saw no one.

He had three coffees while waiting for the first train to Milan; and when he did eventually get on it and take a seat, his stomach felt hollow and outraged, and he had a furry taste in his mouth.

*

For the next seven hours he stared out of the train window. Lazio. Umbria. Tuscany. Emilia. Lombardy. He didn't take his eyes from the passing landscape. He didn't speak to anyone, he didn't look at anyone.

In Milan he had to wait half an hour for a train to Stresa. He drank two more coffees.

At four-thirty he rang the bell of his parents' apartment. His mother opened the door; his small, neat, fat mother. She didn't seem surprised to see him. "Paul, darling," she said. "What a nice surprise."

He wanted to cry. He put his bag down and kissed his mother, then went into the big, high-ceilinged living room overlooking the lake, and said hello to his father—and to his aunt, who was still, apparently, staying there.

He sat down and chatted to his father and aunt while his mother made him some coffee and a sandwich; then he told them all that his concert in Palermo had been canceled for some reason, so he had decided to come and see them. He talked easily. He smiled as he spoke. He almost believed what he said. He felt relaxed, and safe. He was glad he had come. He was glad to see his parents. He was even glad to see his aunt, pompous and stupid though he had always found her.

They all told him how well he was looking. He said he felt well. His father asked him if he was disappointed not to be playing in Palermo, and if he would be paid for the concert. He said yes, rather, and no, probably not.

His aunt laid down her knitting—the wool was violet—and asked him when he was going to get married.

Paolo smiled and said he had been thinking about it recently.

His father grunted that his grandmother's money must have something to do with that. His mother said, "Who to?"

"Oh, an American girl I met."

"What's her name?" his mother asked.

"Maggie."

"Is she rich?" his tall, thin, white-haired father asked.

"Yes she is," Paolo said with a smile.

His aunt made a clicking noise with her tongue; or maybe with her knitting needles.

Paolo felt safe.

When his mother had a chance to speak to him alone she said, "I'm sorry Mary's still here. But if you'd let me know you were coming I'd have found an excuse for sending her home."

"That's okay. I don't really mind her."

"You *are* in a good mood."

Paolo was in a good mood all that evening. His father talked in his high thin voice about money, and about the follies of the Democrats in America, and the follies of the Christian Democrats, the Socialists, the Communists, and almost everyone else in Italy. He smiled drily at Paolo as he talked, as if hoping to shock him. His mother talked about the oddities of the Italian medical services. They both told him that, all things considered, they were very happy that they had come to live in Italy. His aunt talked about the cultural life of Washington, where she lived.

The evening passed pleasantly. Paolo felt that his parents were proud of their good-looking, talented son; and he too felt proud of him—but as if he were some third person.

The next morning he offered to accompany his aunt on her daily steamer trip around the lake. His father said, "Willingly, willingly," and laughed. His mother said, "Paul, dear, are you feeling well?" His aunt seemed offended, as if she had expected the company of both father and son; but she said, "That'll be very kind of you Paul."

He sat on the steamer, next to his big-nosed, big-boned aunt with her tight lacquered hair and her checked suit and pink ruffled blouse; with her large legs crossed and her violet knitting on her knees. She was lecturing him about the political immaturity of artists; telling him how stupid, how negative it was for artists to have any political opinions, or, worse, express them. When she had finished that speech she returned to the cultural life of Washington. Paolo was amazed that there was so much to talk about—though he suspected that, had he listened to her, he would have learned that in fact there wasn't.

But he didn't listen to her droning on as she knitted. He watched the lovely lake slide past, the reflections in the water, the turn-of-the-century towns on the shore. He looked away at the mountains. The morning was clear and warm. He heard, around him, other passengers commenting softly in French, German, Swedish, and Italian on the beauty of the scene.

They had been out on the lake for about half an hour when his aunt majestically laid her knitting down and turned to him and said, "It was very sweet of you to come home yesterday, Paul. I know your mother and father appreciated it very much."

Paolo frowned slightly. He felt she was alluding to something more than his simply turning up as he had.

"Why?" he said.

His aunt laughed briefly and humorlessly. "Oh, you mean you didn't come yesterday on purpose? I was giving you credit for something you didn't deserve, then." She sounded pleased, and resumed her knitting.

"What was yesterday? It wasn't anyone's birthday, was it?"

"Yesterday was the twentieth of October."

Paolo frowned. The date meant nothing to him.

"Your brother died on the twentieth of October six years ago. Your mother was *very* low yesterday."

Paolo looked at the lake. He hated his aunt. Pompous, lying cow. He was sure his mother hadn't been low yesterday; thought-ful, a little sad maybe, but not, as his aunt made it sound, on the verge of suicide. Nevertheless, some of the warmth seemed to pass from the sun. He *had* forgotten—if he had ever known. He thought back to the letter his father had written him, telling him that Kim had died. His father had said, "Yesterday." But the letter hadn't been dated. It had been a scrawl.

But it had been the end of October. His aunt was probably right. The twentieth of October. And he had come home yester-day, the day that his brother had died. His brother, whom he had tried to kill. . . .

He shivered, and looked at the lake that had been alive and soft and warm a minute ago; now it was dead, and hard, and cold. He shivered, and wished that the sun would come out from behind its cloud. Then he froze on his seat next to his aunt and realized that the darkness and cold didn't come from the sun but from behind him. For somewhere among the other passengers who were talking so inanely, so gratingly, was Ralph. He knew it. He could feel the boy's presence, dark and cold and appalling. He didn't dare look around into the dark mad eyes of the cripple; into the eyes of the boy who was sitting behind him with, perhaps, a gun in his pocket, or a long rusty knife concealed under his jacket. Perhaps even how he was moving from his seat. There were not so many people on the boat. Probably there was an empty seat behind him. Ralph was moving up, into it. Ralph with a gun, or with a knife.

Paolo was cold, but he was sweating. He sat rigid in his seat and listened to his aunt telling him that Beethoven was the greatest composer and it wasn't a matter of opinion but a fact, and it was useless to deny it, and didn't Paul agree. . . .

"Yes," Paolo murmured.

. . . After all, look at all he had written, and he was such a tragic man it stood to reason that he was a great composer—she went on, and on, and on, and Paolo hung on her words as if they were a fragile lifeline that could still pull him to safety, could still save him from Ralph, who was sitting behind him somewhere, and was going to kill him.

Paolo murmured "Yes" and "No" at suitable intervals and hoped his aunt's loathsome monologue would never stop. He wished he could say he felt sick, and ask if the boat could turn back, immediately. But he couldn't move. Because if he did there would be confusion; people would stand up, talk, complain, sympathize—and in the confusion Ralph would come up to him, and kill him.

He wondered how long the trip would take. An hour? Two hours? A day. A week. It didn't matter. However long it took would seem to be forever.

He sat there, sweating, shivering.

His aunt stopped talking. He said desperately, "You haven't considered coming to live in Europe?"

"No," the woman snapped. "Not for a moment." She said no more.

Paolo tried, "Do you think that the general level of culture in the States is superior or inferior to that of Europe?"

His aunt paused. Possibly she wondered, for a second, whether

Paolo was making fun of her. But then she swallowed the bait. She couldn't resist depth. She started talking.

The boat went on; but it seemed to be still. Perhaps its engines would break down. Perhaps they had gotten on the wrong boat and it really was going on a whole day trip. Perhaps ... On and on they went, and Paolo never took his eyes off the fat neck of a German tourist sitting in front of him.

Whenever his aunt stopped talking he found a new subject to throw to her. He had to keep her talking. She must talk and talk and talk—or he would have to look around; look around into Ralph's eyes. Give him a nod, or some sign of recognition. Give him the sign that he was ready for him. That he was ready to die.

He could feel his T-shirt, under his sweater, clinging to his back. His back, which any second might be punctured by a bullet, or a knife.

Finally he saw Stresa in front of the steamer. They were going in. Would Ralph do it now? Or perhaps in the jostle and push as they were getting off the boat?

As soon as the other passengers started to stand up and put their cameras away and prepare for landing, Paolo stood up too. He had to be first off. He looked at his aunt. She was still knitting.

"Do sit down, Paul," she said. "There's no rush. I can't understand why everyone always stands up to leap off the boat as soon as we arrive. You'd think they're glad the trip's over. All that pushing. What difference does half a minute make? Sit down."

Paolo sat down, and closed his eyes. He pretended to be asleep. He heard his aunt knitting. He felt the boat shudder as it ran up against the jetty. He heard people moving about, talking, getting off the boat. His aunt was still knitting. It was going to happen now. Now!

But nothing happened. He heard his aunt stop knitting and put her wool and needles in her bag. He opened his eyes. Most of the passengers were already on the jetty, walking away from the boat. Perhaps Ralph had slipped away. Perhaps he had been on the boat to give one last warning. Or was he still, even now, behind him, waiting?

Aunt and nephew stood up, and together they left the boat.

They walked home.

His mother said, "Did you enjoy yourself?"
Paolo winked at her ironically.
He was home again. For another day, at least, he was safe.

He stayed in all that afternoon and read *Great Expectations* for the third time.

That evening his father said to him, "Mary said you were very charming to her." He laughed. "Do you want to take her again tomorrow?"
Paolo smiled. "No, thanks. I've done my duty. I won't deprive you of the joy of your sister's company."
His father grunted.

He stayed in all next day until the late afternoon; then his mother said, "I have to do some shopping. Will you come with me, Paul?"
He went. In the street he looked down at the sidewalk, or at his mother if she spoke. About five minutes after they had set out —they had just come out of a butcher's shop—he shivered. He knew that the cripple was behind him.
He managed to control himself, talking to his mother as if nothing were wrong. But he didn't dare look around; and when, an hour later, he was at home again, he felt sick.
That evening he wasn't hungry, but he ate, so no one would think anything was wrong. After dinner the family sat in the living room; his parents watched the television, his aunt knitted, and he realized that tomorrow he had to send the telegram to Palermo. He felt that he would be confirming a death sentence.

He went to the post office alone. He could feel Ralph behind him. He wrote out a long telegram and paid for it, and as he saw the girl behind the counter take the form and slip it into a pigeon-hole, he turned, ready at last to face Ralph.
He walked out of the post office into the sunny street. He looked up and down.
But there was no sign of Ralph.

He looked more carefully; in doorways, and shops down the street.

There was no one.

He started to walk home. He didn't feel sick any more, just very, very tired. He knew he couldn't stay up here in Stresa any longer. He had to face whatever he had to face. He had to go back to Ralph.

He told his mother that he would be leaving the next day. She said, "Oh, I'm sorry, dear. I've invited some people to dinner to-morrow night who wanted to meet you."

Paolo shrugged. "Okay. I'll go the day after tomorrow."

It didn't matter. He was saying goodbye to the world. Ralph wouldn't begrudge him an extra day. One couldn't leave without saying goodbye.

On the morning of the twenty-fifth he kissed his mother and father, and told them that he would see them at Christmas. He kissed—awkwardly—his aunt, and said he hoped he saw her again before she returned to Washington. Over her shoulder he saw his father smiling drily at him.

He arrived in Rome at eleven o'clock that evening. He made himself a glass of hot milk and went to bed. But he couldn't sleep. Not because he was agitated, or nervous, or frightened. He was simply too tired. After half an hour of lying in bed he took a sleep-ing pill. Another half hour later he took two more.

He slept.

He had a pain in his shoulders. He tried to move, but he couldn't. His arms and hands seemed paralyzed. He felt himself rising slowly to consciousness. He shook his head. He was waking up. He wondered what time it was. He wondered how long he had slept. He shook his head again. Today was October 26, and he should have been in Palermo to give a concert. But he wasn't giving a concert in Palermo, and he couldn't move his arms or hands. He was lying on his stomach and his arms were stretched out straight in front of him. He couldn't move them.

He had a pain in his shoulders, and in his wrists. As he became fully awake he felt a wave of panic wash over him.

He opened his eyes and gasped—though he sounded as if he were about to vomit. His arms were stretched out in front of him because they were handcuffed to the brass rails of his bed head. And his hands were covered in blood.

6

He heard a laugh. Turning his head he saw, across the dark, shuttered room, Ralph squatting on the floor watching him.

"I thought you'd never wake up," the boy said.

Paolo looked at his hands again. He could feel no pain in them. He moved his fingers.

"What've you done?" he croaked.

Ralph smiled.

"How did you get in?"

"Oh, that was easy. The other night when you slept with Maggie I came into the room and took your jacket. I had your keys copied while you were asleep."

"What've you done?" Paolo repeated.

"Nothing yet."

"But the blood—?"

Ralph laughed. "I thought it was going to be difficult getting those handcuffs on you. But you were so deeply asleep it was easy. I just clipped one on your wrist and pulled your arm up and attached it to the rail there, and then you more or less offered me your other arm." He spoke as if he had resolved some technical problem in a car.

"What's the time?"

Ralph looked at his watch. "Just before one."

"How did you know I was here?"

"Maggie telephoned Palermo to find out if you really had canceled your concert. You were sick, they said."

Paolo laid his head on the pillow. He had to think, he told himself. But there was nothing to think about. He was a prisoner. He was helpless.

"What time did you come?"

"At six."

Paolo shivered. His back was cold. He tried to lift his head and look over his shoulders. He had been Ralph's prisoner for almost seven hours. He wondered if the boy had touched him as he had lain asleep, manacled to the bed.

"Are you cold?"

"My back is."

Ralph stood up and hopped over to the bed and pulled the covers up around Paolo's shoulders; gently, as if he were tucking in a child, or an invalid.

"What're you going to do?" Paolo whispered.

"That depends on you," Ralph said in a matter-of-fact way.

"What do I have to do?"

"You know."

"I don't."

"You just have to agree to marry Maggie. Swear it. Make me believe it."

"But it's mad," Paolo whispered.

"Of course it is," Ralph snapped. He sounded very angry. "But what's the point of saying 'It's mad'?" He imitated Paolo's whisper. He walked away from the bed and resumed his squatting position. "It's like saying that the world's round. I *know*. But it doesn't change anything. You either agree to marry Maggie, or—"

"Or?"

Ralph stood up again, and came back to the bed. He knelt down and put his face very close to Paolo's. His lips were wet, and his breath again smelled of garlic. He smiled, and said very quietly, "Or else, dear Paolo, I'm going to eat your hands."

Paolo tried to move away from the boy, but he couldn't. He couldn't move at all. Not even an inch. He was too frightened. He didn't know what to say, so he asked, as he had so many times before, "But why me? Why must I marry Maggie?"

"I've told you."

"But if you love Maggie you can't want her to marry me. You *can't* love me. She can't. It's—" He stopped. He had been going to say, again, "It's mad." He tried to swallow, but he had no saliva in his throat. "You should hate me. I've behaved horribly to you."

Ralph gave a short laugh, and took his face away from Paolo's. He sat on the floor. "Oh, God, you'll make me cry," he said.

"But it's true."

"But it's true," Ralph whined in imitation. "Of course it is. But I expected you to behave as you did. If you hadn't I'd have been disappointed." Again he laughed. "But you'll stop behaving horribly. You have to, don't you?"

"But what about Maggie?"

"Maggie wants to marry you because she doesn't want me to kill you. And also because, in spite of everything, she likes you, and thinks that in normal circumstances—which she hopes will come soon—she'll get to love you. She finds you physically attractive. And then she loves music, and thinks if you married her she could help you to become a great pianist, instead of just a good one, which you are now. She thinks it's a shame that you're so messed up you don't play as you could." He added, ironically, "That you don't fulfill yourself."

"I could never love Maggie. I like her, but—I can't marry her."

"*She* thinks that if you really got to love the music you played, instead of just yourself playing it—if you really understood what you were playing—then you would start to love her." He sounded amused, and sarcastic.

"And if I married Maggie, what would you do?"

"Oh, don't worry about me. After you've married Maggie I'll look after myself." Ralph looked away toward the wall. In a small voice he said, "I think if you were really happy I'd kill myself."

Paolo tried to speak reasonably, calmly, and kindly. He said, "I can't marry Maggie, Ralph, and I'm not going to. And now please take these handcuffs off me."

Ralph jumped up and grabbed his hair, and lifted his head off the pillow. He hissed, "You are going to marry Maggie." Then he stopped, and rolled his mouth around. Paolo closed his eyes. He heard and felt the spit on his face. Ralph let go of his hair, and his head dropped. He wiped it on the pillow as best he could.

"You fake," Ralph murmured. "You cheap filthy fake murderer."

Paolo raised his head and stared at the boy.

Ralph was trembling. "How dare you try and be all calm and reasonable with me. You! If I hadn't seen you at that concert, or if I hadn't been feeling in a good mood that night, or whatever it was—if I hadn't wanted you then you'd be dead by now. You know that, don't you?"

Paolo didn't reply. He continued to stare at the boy, who suddenly lowered his eyes and blushed, and muttered, "I'm sorry."

Again he took hold of Paolo's hair and lifted his head; but this time, with his free hand, and with a corner of the sheet, he started to wipe his face.

"What do you mean?" Paolo said.

"Oh, you know what I mean. You must. You can't be that stupid. Why do you think I came to Italy? Why do you think I wanted to kill you before I ever saw you?"

"I'm sorry, Ralph, but I am stupid. I don't know. I didn't know that you had."

Ralph shivered. "Do you have a heater? I'm cold."

"There's one over there in the bottom of the wardrobe."

Ralph went over to the wardrobe and took out the heater and plugged it in the wall. He put it near the bed. For the first time, Paolo noticed that the boy was wearing the clothes he had first seen him in; cord trousers and baggy sweater and tweed jacket. It made him, for some reason, feel even more frightened.

"That's better," Ralph said. He looked at Paolo, and touched the steel rings around his wrists.

"Whose blood do you think that is on your hands?"

"I don't know."

"Then I guess you are that stupid. Everything Maggie's told you. Everything that's happened—" He touched one of Paolo's hands with a finger, and put the red finger in his mouth. "Or you think we're stupid. I suppose that's it. You think that because we're mad we're also stupid." He sighed. "But you see, Paolo, I always read the newspapers. Especially the crime reports. I expect Maggie's told you. She never does. She just reads the headlines and the articles about music. But I *saw* those reports in two or three different papers. Just little paragraphs, but I didn't tell Maggie for more than two months—until I knew what I was going to do. And then I was waiting for that letter. I *knew* it was going to come. Christopher told me."

"Oh," Paolo breathed. "Christopher."

"Yes! Christopher. Christopher. Christopher. My God, Paolo, you're not stupid. You're deficient. Who did you think Maggie had been going to marry? Who did you think I'd fallen in love with in London, and wanted Maggie to marry? Who do you think told us all about you? Why do you think we came to Italy for you?"

"Oh," Paolo breathed again. The world had slipped away from under him. He was in dark, weightless space, and he was utterly, completely exhausted. He lay there and thought of all that Maggie had told him. Of all that had happened in the last month. Yes. He had been stupid. Perhaps a part of him had realized, but he had refused to let himself draw any conclusions from the co-incidences, from the pattern. Of course Christopher was the only explanation. Christopher was the explanation of everything.

"I didn't kill Christopher," he whispered to Ralph. "We talked a lot, but he was responsible for his own death. I might have talked him into doing something, but it was Christopher who decided to take his own life. No one can decide that for someone else. He was weak."

Ralph said nothing, and Paolo looked at him.

"Christopher left Maggie *all* his money?"

Ralph nodded. He had tears in his eyes. But then he laughed. "Why? Did you think you were going to get it? Is that why you killed him?"

"Ralph, you don't think I actually went there and murdered him, do you?"

The thin boy put his head on one side and said, "I don't think, Paolo. I *know*."

"I didn't. I swear I didn't." He heard that he was shouting, and felt sweat break out on his forehead.

Again, with the corner of the sheet, Ralph gently wiped Paolo's face.

"I just didn't know why," he said. "But I guess if you thought Christopher had left you all his money, that's it. But you see, in Christopher's last letter, he begged Maggie to forgive him and everything. But he wrote another letter, to me, saying that he had—or was going to—make a new will leaving everything to Maggie—and he said, 'So if anything happens to me, at least I'll have done something I hope is good, and something which I hope will prove to Maggie that I did love her and will maybe make her forgive me.' He knew something was going to happen to him."

"He must have been thinking about suicide then."

"Did he tell you he was making a new will?"

"Yes."

"And I guess you thought he was going to leave everything to you." Ralph laughed.

"No. I didn't. I—" Paolo closed his eyes.

"You did."

"Perhaps."

"Were you disappointed when you never heard anything?"

"No. Of course not. I never thought about it for a moment."

"Don't be ridiculous. Of course you did. Everyone always does. Maybe just an idle fantasy, but *something*."

"Well, maybe just an idle fantasy. But nothing more. Christopher told me he was going to make a new will—but I thought he probably hadn't, after all, or—I don't know." He stopped and told himself that what he had said was true, even if Ralph didn't believe him. Yes—he had thought that Christopher was going to leave him his money. But then when Christopher had died, Paolo hadn't allowed himself to wait expectantly for a letter from a lawyer, to wonder what he would do with the money, to be disappointed when he had heard nothing. He had simply wondered occasionally, and without malice, if not he, who had received the fortune. More than that would have been against his belief that —as he had told Christopher—to love money was to hate oneself.

He said, "I didn't kill Christopher, Ralph. Truly."

"Maggie doesn't know you did," Ralph said. "She thinks *I* killed Christopher. That's why she doesn't doubt that I'll kill you. She thinks I'm half crazy, but she feels very philosophical about it —especially since Christopher left her. She thinks you persuaded Christopher to leave her, and she thinks I killed Christopher to avenge her. So she feels guilty about it too. You know, the police came around to our flat in London one day about a week after I'd seen the report in the paper and asked a few questions. Maggie was at work. They said it was in connection with our residency permits, but I knew what it really was. After all, it made Maggie look suspicious, didn't it? Christopher leaving her all his money and then promptly dying like that. I told them in a roundabout way that Maggie had been in the office all the day Christopher had died, and when they saw me I guess they thought *I* couldn't have gone to Italy and killed Christopher. But I told them where I had been that day, just in case, and anyway lots of people had seen me, and they don't forget a freak easily, do they?"

"Did Christopher talk about me a lot?"

"He didn't often talk about anyone else. He told us about your apartment and your character and your habits and what you thought and—everything."

"I didn't kill Christopher," Paolo repeated. "I swear it."

"He told us that he loved you," Ralph said, almost inaudibly. Then he smiled and added, in a normal voice, "You realize that if you marry Maggie you'll get Christopher's money in any case. That'll be ironic, won't it?"

"I didn't murder Christopher and I'm not going to marry Maggie."

"You did and you are."

"Ralph—be logical. I could marry her even less now. Think of it from my point of view. If I agreed to marry Maggie it would be like an admission. It would look as though I were doing it because I did kill Christopher."

Ralph laughed. "Yes, it would, wouldn't it? That's why you're going to."

Paolo started sweating again. But he was no longer frightened. He was angry. He pulled himself up until his head was pressed against the brass railings. He looked to see if there was any way of freeing his hands. But while he was looking he heard Ralph stand up; he felt him pull the bedclothes off him, grab hold of his ankles, and jerk him back down the bed. He gasped as the steel handcuffs bit into his wrists. He tried to kick out at Ralph, but he made no contact.

He saw the boy take hold of the side of the bed and drag it into the middle of the room. He saw him turn the light on. Then Ralph came over and knelt at the head of the bed, his face on the other side of the brass railings, only an inch or so from the ends of the bloody fingers. Only now Paolo saw, in the bright electric light, that it was not blood on his fingers. "What is this stuff?"

Ralph giggled. "I didn't think you'd think it was blood for as long as you did. I just wanted to give you a shock when you woke up."

"What is it?"

"Tomato ketchup, of course." The boy giggled again. "I've told you. I'm going to eat your hands unless you do what I want."

For a second Paolo felt that he was balancing on the edge of a pit. He felt that if he could keep his balance he would be able to call Ralph's bluff; reduce the situation to a farce. He should say, "Go on, eat them, then." And watch, as the boy, unable to do it, backed away.

But even as he thought of himself at the edge he was looking at Ralph's face, and losing his balance. He stared at the soft wet lips, at the dark eyes; he smelled that garlic; and he fell. He started struggling, flinging himself from side to side on the bed; but all he achieved was to hurt his wrists more. His fingers remained an inch from Ralph's soft wet lips.

"Just tell me," the boy said thickly, lasciviously. "Just tell me that you killed Christopher and will marry Maggie."

Paolo jerked his head to one side. "I didn't and I won't." He heard his voice, strange, and high, and harsh, and coming from a long way away.

"*Please,*" Ralph said; his voice, too, was in the distance. Paolo could feel the sweat on his bare back, buttocks, and legs. The heater was burning him.

"For Christ's sake, let me go."

"Say it."

"No."

"Say it!"

"No!" He had tears in his eyes. His body was burning. His shoulders ached. His wrists hurt.

Ralph jumped up and ran out of the room. Paolo heard him in the kitchen. Then he saw him coming back, with some things in his hand, and a kitchen knife. He saw through tear-obscured eyes that Ralph was crying too.

The boy knelt again at the head of the bed and put the things he had been carrying on the floor. Paolo looked down. Mustard. Salt. Pepper. The boy was laughing. It *was* a farce. A hideous farce. But the boy was crying, too, and trembling, and he smeared, with the knife, great yellow lumps of mustard onto the tomato-covered hands, so that they looked like terrible wounded birds, with pus seeping from them. Then Ralph started shaking white salt onto the hands that were flapping, faintly, like broken wings. Then black pepper.

Paolo heard himself say very slowly and clearly, "Ralph, you cannot eat my hands," and he wanted to scream—with fear, but also with laughter at the obscene farce. It was hilarious. He managed to pull himself up into a kneeling position, and he realized he must look as if he were praying to Ralph. He could no longer see.

"This is your last chance," Ralph whispered. "Say it. Please, please say it, Paolo. If you don't you're going to die. You know that, don't you? I'm not joking. When they find you your hands will have been eaten, and you'll have bled to death. Please say it. Please. I love you."

"No," Paolo said.

He felt the boy's soft lips sucking the three middle fingers of his right hand into his mouth. He felt the teeth close on his fingers. He screamed, but only what sounded like a dry cough came from his mouth.

"All right, Ralph," he said. "I swear it. I'll marry Maggie."

He felt the teeth release his fingers. He felt the mouth slipping away from them. He heard Ralph stand up. He heard him hop out of the room. He heard the front door open and close. Then there was silence.

He was alone.

He lay on his bed, wet, trembling, and crying.

He lay there for an hour. He didn't struggle, or try to free himself. He knew that Ralph couldn't leave him there to die of starvation or thirst. Sooner or later the boy would return, and release him. Release him for what? For Maggie. He would never be free again.

*

He heard the front door opening and looked up. He felt ashamed; like a child who has behaved badly, been punished, is about to be forgiven, but still feels guilty about his behavior. Also, like a child, he knew that earlier, in his fear, he had wet his bed.

However, it wasn't Ralph who came into the room, but Maggie. She paused for a moment in the doorway and looked at him, then ran over and knelt down in front of him. She had a bunch of keys in her hand, and with one of them she undid the handcuffs. Then she bowed her head and whispered, "Oh, Paolo, I'm so sorry."

Paolo said nothing. He got off the bed and walked slowly to the bathroom. He filled the basin with hot water, and started to wash his hands. He changed the water, washed his hands again, and then rinsed them. He looked at them. Only on the middle finger of his right hand was there the faint mark of a tooth. But he had red weals around his wrists. He took a shower.

He went back into the bedroom and sat, next to Maggie, on the floor.

"Do put some clothes on," she said. "You'll catch cold."

Paolo rested his head on his knees. "I've been roasting in front of the heater for an hour," he said. His stomach felt weak, and he was afraid he was going to start crying again. He told himself to relax, and started to breathe in deeply and regularly. Eventually he said, "Do you know why Ralph wants me to marry you? He thinks I murdered Christopher."

"Oh, no," Maggie said sharply. "He thinks you persuaded Christopher to leave me. That's why he wanted to kill you too. He blamed you for it. But he killed Christopher first."

"He didn't kill Christopher, Maggie. Ralph's never killed anyone. Christopher killed himself, and Ralph let you believe that he did so you'd think he was serious about killing me."

"But he is serious."

"I know. Because he thinks *I* killed Christopher. But *you* came to Italy with Ralph because you believed that he thought I had talked Christopher into leaving you, Ralph had actually killed him, and you didn't want him to kill me. You came to protect me in some way. Or rather to protect Ralph from himself, because I guess you hated me." He shrugged. "Still do, probably. Only then

Ralph saw me at the concert and fell in love with me, and so gave you the opportunity to save me—by marrying me. That way everyone would have been saved. But then you had to make up all those other things—so it seemed you weren't just making some absurd sacrifice, but really wanted me. You had to fool yourself and say all that about my music, and feeling sorry for me, to make me bearable."

"I didn't make those things up, Paolo. They're true. But if Ralph didn't kill Christopher, why didn't he tell me that he thought you had? Why didn't he just come here and kill you and then come home and tell me what he'd done?"

"I guess because he'd never killed anyone he thought he might not be able to go through with it."

"Then he could have come back to England and not said anything."

"But he wanted to do something for you. To avenge you. Only he was frightened. He came here to kill me"—Paolo paused —"but he brought you because he must have hoped, secretly, that there'd be a way out, and he wouldn't have to kill anyone. He didn't really want to. When he saw me at that concert he wanted to fall in love with me. It was the perfect solution. He didn't have to kill anybody, you'd be happy, he hoped—even with Christopher's murderer—and you'd both have your revenge on me." He stopped, and said quietly, "But you do believe me when I say I didn't kill Christopher?"

"Yes," Maggie whispered. She sat on the floor, trying to take in everything he had told her. Then she said, "But why did Christopher kill himself, Paolo?"

"I honestly don't know. But I think it was because he had let himself be persuaded to leave you. Or because he had left you."

"He could have come back. I would have forgiven him."

"But he wouldn't have forgiven himself."

There was a long silence, which Maggie finally broke. "He was in love with you, wasn't he?"

Paolo nodded. Then he said, "Will you—would you—ever be able to forgive *me*?"

"No," Maggie said decisively. "Never. That's why you've got

to marry me. I'll never forgive you. But I think I might love you," she added nervously.

"Ralph made me swear I'd marry you."

"He told me." She touched him on the shoulder, and he turned to her. "And will you now?"

Paolo took her hand and held it. "I don't know. Because if I did Ralph would take it as an admission that I killed Christopher."

"Do you care what he thinks?"

"Yes. Because—if only I could prove to him that I didn't, I don't think he would insist on my marrying you." He smiled, sadly, at Maggie. "If I could prove my innocence, I could go free."

"And if not, you're stuck with me." Maggie, too, smiled. "Poor Paolo. But I do want to marry you, and I hope you never will prove anything. I don't see how you can, in any case." She looked down at the floor. "Do you hate me, Paolo?"

Paolo thought for a while before replying. Finally he said, "No. I should have thought that was obvious. I mean—I really like you. Only I don't want to marry you."

"And if we did—have to get married, would you hate me?"

"No. I don't think so."

"You'd hate Ralph."

Again Paolo thought before replying. "I don't know if I'd even do that. I think I'd probably just hate myself for having got into this insane situation." He stopped, and raised his eyebrows. "But you must do me a favor. If by any dreadful chance we were forced to get married because of Ralph, please don't ever forget I'll have done it only because I was forced to. Please don't ever pretend about anything. And please don't ever tell me that you love me."

Maggie gazed at him as if she hadn't understood him; but she murmured, "All right."

"What would Ralph do if we *did* get married?"

Maggie was still gazing at him; then she lowered her eyes and shrugged. "Oh, I don't know. He can live somewhere. I'd give him an allowance."

"He'd live by himself?"

"Of course. I mean—I suppose."

Paolo lay flat on the floor. He closed his eyes. He said, "I think if we did get married and he thought we'd stay married he'd kill himself."

Maggie stretched out beside him. "Yes," she said. "I think he might." She spoke so quietly Paolo hardly heard her.

"Would you mind?"

"Of course I'd mind. But you know—in an awful way I'd be relieved. That's terrible, isn't it?" She rolled onto her side, and with a hand turned his face. She looked into his eyes. "If you married me and then Ralph killed himself, would you leave me?"

"I don't know." He looked at the pale, intense face, with its brown curly hair. "But if Ralph did kill himself I have a feeling that he'd do it in some way—I don't know how—that would—tie us. I don't know how."

They lay on the floor together, thinking.

"Why didn't you tell me it was Christopher you were going to marry? Why did you tell me all that story as if it had nothing to do with me?"

"Ralph told me not to. He wanted to be the one to tell you, if you didn't guess without being told. You should have."

"Yes."

"Ralph's planned everything. The trip abroad, the whole mise-en-scene. It's all been him." She smiled. "He's the author and director and everything else of the entire show."

"Ralph thinks I killed Christopher for his money."

"Oh. Well, if you did you lost out there, didn't you?"

"Ralph says not. Because if I marry you—"

"Oh, I hadn't thought of that. I guess he's right. Maybe that's how he's planning to keep us together."

They lay side by side on the floor. Paolo rested his head on Maggie's shoulder, and gradually fell asleep.

He didn't sleep for long, as far as he could tell. When he woke Maggie said she had to leave him; she wanted to go home and see how Ralph was.

Paolo decided to go to see Elaine.

He went around to her apartment, rang her bell, walked in when she opened the door, and then, without giving her a chance to speak, started telling her everything that had happened; everything, from Christopher's return to Rome to the events of that morning.

When he had finished Elaine exclaimed, "How exciting, Paolo! Why didn't you tell me before?"

"I couldn't. It was all a nightmare before. There was no reason in it, no logic. I couldn't tell anyone. I wanted to. I wanted to explain. But everything was inexplicable. I thought I was going mad. But now—now I see it's all to do with Christopher, there's an explanation for everything. I feel I can cope with it."

"So you're going to marry this Maggie?"

"I don't know." He smiled. "What do you think?"

"I don't see how you can avoid it." She laughed. "How funny! What'll happen to the brother if you do?"

"I don't know. I asked Maggie that. She said he'll go away."

"Well, if he does you can leave her."

"I think he might kill himself. He said he might—"

"Perfect!"

"I told Maggie. She didn't seem to mind the idea."

"She'd probably be relieved."

"She said she would, in a way."

"There you are. She wants to marry you to get rid of her brother."

"Maybe. In a way." Paolo laughed. "I might have to marry her in any case. Because if I don't, and things go on as they are, I won't be able to play any more, and I won't earn any money. She'll have to support me." He felt, strangely, lightheaded and excited. "Let's go out to dinner," he said.

They went out to dinner at seven-thirty. Paolo was hungry; he hadn't eaten anything all day. They ate, and laughed, and talked about Maggie, and Ralph, and Elaine's marriage. It was like the old times, before Maggie and Ralph. Like the old times—only as the evening wore on Paolo's excitement, instead of mellowing with the food and wine, increased. At eleven o'clock he said to Elaine, "I'm going to leave you now."

"Where are you going?"

"I don't know. For a walk, I think."

"You're going to see her, aren't you?" Elaine said sourly. She pushed her lank hair off her face and added in a flat voice, "I think you're in love with her."

"Rubbish. She's a secretary. Or an ex-secretary."

Elaine shrugged her shoulders. She looked old, sad, and haggard. "I guess this is our farewell dinner."

Paolo stared at her and, for a moment, felt sorry for her. But only for a moment. He stared at her and wondered if, under other circumstances, he might have been able to help her. But he thought not. Their friendship was hopeless. He smiled at her. She was right. This was their farewell dinner. They had nothing more to say to each other. He had come to see her just for old times' sake; the new times promised him something different.

"Well, I wish you luck," Elaine said. "Better luck than *I* had."

He took one last look at her bitter mouth and tiny fingers. At helpless, hopeless Elaine.

He signaled the waiter and asked for the bill.

As he was paying, Elaine said, "They're very clever, those two. The brother's clever, but she's cleverer. He's in love with you and wants you to marry his sister so he can be at ease with himself and forgive you for Christopher—and get some sort of vicarious thrill. And she says she wants to marry you to save you from her brother and because she wants to get married and because she likes music. But really why she wants to marry you is because if she does she'll get rid of her brother. *You'll* get rid of her brother for her. She knows you're capable of it. If Christopher had married her, after six months they'd all have been living together— the brother would have said he was lonely, and threatened to kill himself, and Maggie would have said come and live with us. And Christopher would have agreed. She knows that. And I'm sure that she thinks that's the real reason why Christopher left her— whatever he wrote her. And she might be right.

"Your persuasion was incidental. Christopher wanted to be persuaded. He got in touch with you when he came here to pack up just so he could be persuaded. And writing you and telling you that he loved you was just an excuse for him. A way out. The real cause of his wanting to leave Maggie was that he couldn't bear the idea of marrying the two of them." She was speaking so fast Paolo could hardly catch her words. The waiter stood by the table looking at the notes Paolo held in his hand. She rushed on. "But you're stronger than Christopher. You'll really get rid of Ralph. Send him to the other end of the earth, or persuade him to kill himself. And when you've done that *she'll* be free, and you"—Elaine barked a laugh—"will be in love with her—with your ex-secretary—and you'll be stuck. You see, Paolo? She's the one who's going to come out of all this on top. How's that for irony?"

Paolo finished counting out his money, and gave it to the waiter.

"Come on," he said. "I'll put you in a taxi."

When Elaine was gone, Paolo stood in the street and wondered what to do. He was excited. He wanted to have sex. He thought of what Elaine had said, and smiled to himself. He took a taxi to Via Francesco Crispi. Maggie opened the door to him. She looked as if she'd been expecting him.

They made love four times that night. The first time they were almost shy with each other, as if they were two virgins on the first night of their marriage. But then they both relaxed.

At four o'clock in the morning Maggie whispered, "We'll be so happy, Paolo. We will, really. You'll play and you'll be great and we'll be happy and Ralph will be happy."

Five minutes later Paolo said, "Do you really love Ralph?"

"Oh, yes. Really. More than I could ever love you or anyone, I think. He's been the whole of my life. In a way he's almost me, and I'm almost him. But in spite of that—or because of that"—she hesitated—"I'd love to be free of him."

Soon after that the girl went to sleep, but Paolo lay awake in the darkness, and, in spite of his physical exhaustion, was more excited than ever. He had wanted to have sex; he had had it. But he was still excited. He lay awake; and finally the reason for his excitement came to him. He wanted to get rid of Ralph. He was going to get rid of Ralph.

He wanted to kill Ralph.

7

Paolo left Maggie the next morning and went home. He had to make a plan, and it had to be simple. Something as simple as pushing his baby brother off a roof.

He didn't have to think for long before he realized what he was going to do; and it was more than simple. It was perfect. It almost amounted to Ralph killing himself, which he had said he might do in any case.

How would Ralph kill himself, if he did? If he was sure that Paolo and Maggie were going to be happy together, what death would he plan for himself? There was no doubt in Paolo's mind. Ralph would put a glove on his right hand, put the gun that he kept by his bed to his head, and pull the trigger. He would want to die as Christopher had died, and in memory of Christopher.

And so he would.

But first other things must be done, Paolo thought. Above all, he must clear himself, in advance, of any suspicion regarding Ralph's death. Clear himself, not only as far as the police were concerned, but also as far as Maggie was concerned. And to do that he would have to persuade the girl that suddenly, without knowing how, he fallen in love with her. Elaine believed he was in love with her already, so she could give evidence if evidence were needed. He would convince Maggie that he loved her, and convince Ralph. He would fix a day for the wedding. He would start getting the necessary documents together. He would start looking for an apartment with Maggie; an unfurnished place, that they could decorate together, that would be a home for them. He would appear so changed, so happy, that Ralph would think he had won; that it was time for him to leave the lovers for their life together; that he should kill himself.

Maggie might think it strange Ralph hadn't waited until after the wedding; but she wouldn't think it too strange. And even if she did she would say nothing. For she wanted to be free of him herself.

The plan was perfect.

As far as he could see, there was only one other thing to be taken care of. If Ralph died in precisely the same way that Christopher had died, the police might connect the two cases, and suspicion for Ralph's death—and possibly even Christopher's death—might fall on Maggie or himself. And as Maggie and he had already been—if only very vaguely—suspected of that first death, to clear themselves of the second might be more difficult.

Paolo thought, for a moment, that it would be even more perfect if Maggie *was* suspected. But he dismissed the thought. If he did that, the affair would become less simple; darker, and more dangerous.

No. It had to be clear, without any doubts, that Ralph had killed himself. Maggie and he must have watertight alibis.

He made some lunch and, after he had eaten, went to lie down on his bed. He looked at his photographs, and they glowed, and were golden. He felt that he had never been more brilliant than he was now, never greater. Great by his own definition—which was the only valid, true definition.

By five o'clock he had worked out all the details of his plan. It occurred to him once that if anything should go wrong he would be in a far worse position than if he simply married Maggie and did what Ralph told him. But he was sure that nothing could go wrong. Everything was too simple. Too perfect.

That evening he started to put the plan into action.

He went to Maggie's at eight o'clock, and they had a drink together. He told her that he had been practicing all afternoon.

"When's your next concert?"

"Not till December fifteenth. But then after that I have another on December twenty-eighth, another on January twelfth, another on January thirtieth, and two in February. And so on, through the spring. Only one a month after February, thank God. But I've got dates up to September of next year."

Maggie nodded.

Paolo said, "I've got to talk to you about all that. And—everything."

Maggie smiled. "I'm listening."

Paolo looked around, as if afraid that Ralph might overhear him.

"He's out," Maggie said.

"Well, let's go out ourselves and have some dinner. Then it'll be easier to talk."

As they took the elevator down Paolo kissed Maggie. He was excited. He wanted to make love to her.

"What's wrong with you?" Maggie said.

"I don't know. Last night I had dinner with Elaine and I got excited during the dinner and—well, you know. I've been excited ever since. I don't know why."

Maggie seemed puzzled.

Paolo said truthfully, "I've never been like this before. I'm not really a very—how shall I say—sexual person. Sometimes I think I'm becoming impotent. Sometimes I don't have anything for more than a month. Two, even. And it doesn't worry me."

The elevator arrived at the ground floor. As the doors opened Paolo said, "Did you and Christopher make love?"

"Of course." The tall girl blushed. She looked embarrassed, and slightly annoyed.

Paolo wanted to ask her what it had been like, but he guessed he couldn't. For all Maggie's strangeness, she was a very ordinary girl, with very ordinary prejudices, he was sure.

"It was beautiful," Maggie said softly.

They went to a restaurant. As they sat holding hands waiting for their order, Paolo said, "Do you always wear black because of Christopher?"

"Yes. Stupid, isn't it?"

"Will you change one day?"

"Oh, yes. One day I'll burst out all in white." She smiled and, for the second time that evening, blushed. "You know, when the first of the money arrived I went out and bought myself a white mink coat. I don't know why. I'm not really the type. But I thought I should do it and see if I enjoyed spending money. I didn't. I didn't exactly feel guilty. Just stupid." Again she blushed. "It's probably because of that that I only wear black. Because having spent all that money on that coat and never having worn it I feel it's ridiculous to go out and buy any more clothes which I might not wear. Perhaps if and when I do start wearing the coat I'll go wild and buy a whole new wardrobe. But, you see, it's difficult for me. I've had to be so careful about money all my life that I don't feel at ease spending it."

Paolo squeezed her hand. "You're absolutely mad. When did you buy the coat?"

"In the middle of August, in London."

"Well, how could you have worn it? It hasn't been the weather for fur coats yet."

Maggie smiled, shyly. "Do you know, I hadn't really thought of that. But that's another thing. Ralph and I normally lived so much at home, or at least together, that somehow the outside world didn't often touch us. Things like seasons—I don't know. I hardly noticed them. I suppose that's why we're so pale. And I suppose that's another reason why I bought the coat then. I got it the day before Ralph came back. I'd been alone for two months by then. I was beginning to have to cope with the outside world. I didn't know if he was ever coming back."

"You wait till it gets cold here. Then you'll wear it and won't feel guilty, and you'll be able to cope with the outside world by then."

Maggie frowned slightly. "But black suits me," she said.

They had finished their spaghetti when Maggie said, "Why didn't you want Christopher to marry me?"

"I didn't know it was you. Christopher never mentioned any names." He paused. "I told him I didn't want to know your name, or anything about you. You were just the girl he was going to marry."

"But why didn't you want him to marry? You weren't in love with him, were you?"

Paolo looked into her dark, grave eyes and murmured, "Oh, no. But first of all, I didn't think Christopher should marry anyone. I didn't think he was the type. I still don't think he was. Because in a way he was rather like me. I was sure he was doing it to convince himself of something, and it irritated me. It made me angry. It was so weak and stupid and unnecessary. And then I guess—I don't know—but I had the idea that because Christopher was like me in a way he could have been whatever he wanted. But he had to do it by himself." He looked down at the table. "This'll probably sound mad to you, and I can't really explain what I mean, but I just felt that Christopher could have been *great* if he'd wanted to be."

"Because of his money?"

Paolo looked up at her again. "I don't think it was because of that," he said quietly.

"Poor Paolo." Now Maggie looked down at the table. "You were wrong, weren't you?"

"Yes, I guess I was." He corrected himself. "No, I don't guess. I know. I was wrong."

As they were eating their fish, Maggie said, "Paolo, are you going to marry me?"

Paolo looked past Maggie, with his fork in his hand. Then at Maggie. Then he nodded.

"I told you I had dinner with Elaine last night, and that I got so excited I had to leave her? I didn't tell her where I was going, but she knew. She went through a whole jealous scene." He put his fork into a piece of fish. "She told me that I loved you."

"And what did you say?"

"Rubbish."

"So why are you telling me?" Maggie said. But she smiled.

As they were drinking their coffee Paolo said, "Can we talk now? About—you know."

Maggie avoided his eyes and said, "Yes."

"It's so difficult, because we've got to talk about something mad, but we've got to pretend it isn't. We've got to pretend that it's completely normal." He sighed. "But that's the point, Maggie. It is going to be normal. I mean, when we get married, we're going to be married. Regardless of Ralph. Regardless of anyone. We'll be married, and we'll see each other every day, and we'll see other people together, we'll have friends, we'll have a completely normal life. You'll have habits that irritate me, and I'll have habits that irritate you. And we'll have to get used to each other, and pretend—even if it isn't true—that we're together because we like to be together. Not because Ralph's waiting in the wings somewhere to take a shot at me if I leave you."

"You told me the exact opposite yesterday. You told me I should never pretend."

Now Paolo felt like blushing. He had made his first mistake, but it was a small one. He could bluff his way out of it. "Yes, I know I did. But I was thinking last night—this morning—after you'd gone to sleep, that I hadn't really meant that—or yes, in a way I did, but I put it badly. I guess what I should have said was that we should never forget what caused all this situation. But we'll *have* to pretend."

Maggie didn't look convinced.

Paolo went on. "Anyway, listen. Even if I did say that yesterday, I've changed my mind today because I've thought about it more rationally—as rationally as it can be thought of. We *are* going to have to pretend, and you know it, whatever I say. At least for the beginning. After that perhaps we really will like living together. But if we are going to have to pretend we should start right now. Right this minute. Pretend that there are no external pressures on us, and that we're doing exactly what we want to do. We've got to exclude the madness right now, and live as if it didn't exist, and never had. We've got to decide exactly when we're going to get married, and start making applications and getting documents together. I know a lawyer here. He can help us. We'll have to do a few things ourselves, but—"

"Okay." Maggie said expressionlessly.

"The other thing we've got to consider is work. Look. I've got to practice, and play, and give concerts. The one I was supposed to do yesterday was the first one I've ever canceled in my life. I can't ever do that again. Apart from the fact that I don't get paid, it's bad for my reputation. People hear about these things. So I've got to work and practice regularly—and recently, with everything going on, it's been impossible. We've got to get everything settled so I can practice and not be disturbed. We've got to get a place together, and—"

"And we've got to make some arrangements for Ralph. Is that what you're trying to tell me?"

"Yes."

"Well, how would it be if you came to live with me while we're looking for something else—have your piano and things moved over—and let Ralph stay in your place?"

"I had thought of that."

"Well?"

"I don't think it's a very good idea. Not right at this moment. Because Ralph *would* be around, even if I didn't see him. If you went out I'd know you were with him. I'd be conscious of him the whole time."

"But I can't just give Ralph up completely."

"Of course not. But I thought—for a month or two. Just while we're—well, getting to know each other. It would be much better if we went somewhere where we could be completely on our own. Where I can forget about Ralph altogether. Then after a couple of months things between us should be sort of normal. We can come back to Rome and we'll arrange the apartments like you said, and you can go and see Ralph and he'll be just like an ordinary brother-in-law."

"You want us to leave Rome?"

"Only for a couple of months. A month and a half even. Till my next concert. That's on December the fifteenth. Then once that's over we'll come back and—let's say we'll get married on the twentieth of December. How does that sound?"

"I honestly don't know. I mean—oh, I guess I've realized that we'll have to have a normal life together. Only I haven't had much experience in leading a normal life, and now that I've got to it it's sort of frightening. But I want to," Maggie said, urgently.

"It'll be frightening for both of us."

They were silent for a while; then Paolo said, "Anyway, ask Ralph, and see what he thinks. I'm sure he'll see it's the best thing to do. He won't mind being on his own. And he'll know where we are in case of absolute emergency."

"Where will we be?"

"I thought—I've got a friend who has a house in Praiano, next to Positano. He only ever goes there in the summer. It's small, but it's comfortable. There's heat and everything. There's a woman from the village who comes up twice a week when he's not there, to keep an eye on things. When he's there she comes up every day. I'm sure she'd come up for us."

"I don't know if I want to have a woman from the village. I think I'd like to do everything."

Paolo smiled. "You'll get over that. It'll be like your fur coat."

"Is there a piano there?"

"Yes. My friend's a pianist. Not very good, but the piano's excellent. The only thing I'd have to do would be to get someone to come and tune it. But there's someone he knows in Salerno who'll come up."

"When would we leave?"

"Well, first I'd have to check that the house is free, but I'm sure it is. He's offered it to me other times. Then—as soon as possible. If we really rushed around we could probably get all the documents signed and witnessed or whatever we have to do for"—he raised his eyebrows—"our wedding, in a day or two. I'd say in three days' time we could leave."

Maggie looked appalled.

"Or I could go on down and you could join me when you're ready. Next week. Whenever Ralph's been settled. But I've *got* to do something, Maggie. It's more than a month now since I've really practiced. And I must."

Maggie nodded.

"It'll be best like this. I promise." He lowered his voice. "There's one more thing. I generally give five hours of private lessons a week from the beginning of November. Normally they've fitted into my schedule. But I haven't got a schedule any more, and basically they're a waste of time. Only they pay very well. If we go down to Praiano I'm going to have to give those lessons up." He hoped he was looking frankly at Maggie. "Now let's be frank. You're rich, and we're not going to have money problems, so there's no point in my being sentimental and pretending I have to support myself exclusively by giving concerts. I could, quite easily, only these private lessons are a sort of extra security. When we're married I won't need that extra security, and as they are a waste of time, it's better to stop them." He paused. "Do you agree with me?"

Maggie looked confused, and was obviously trying to

absorb all the implications of what he had said. But when she did answer, she sounded decisive. "Yes, of course I agree," she said.

Paolo felt pleased with himself. He had been very clever, he thought. If he had simply told Maggie that he was resigned—even pleasantly resigned—to marrying her, and wanted to go down to Praiano with her so they could start their life together immediately, she would have been happy. Only she might not have believed him. She might secretly, deep down, have doubted his sincerity. She might have believed that that date he had fixed —December 20—would be put back and put back and finally put off altogether. She might have thought that he still planned and hoped to escape her and Ralph.

But now, with the merest suggestion that he wasn't indifferent to her money—to Christopher's money—though she might not be so happy, she would believe him. And the more she thought about it, and talked to Ralph about it, the more she would become convinced that he was marrying her *only* for her money; and the more she and Ralph would believe that he was marrying her with the intention of staying married to her.

He wanted to laugh. The world was marvelous when greed was the only proof of sincerity.

He went home with Maggie, and he was still so excited that, after they had set an alarm for nine-thirty, they made love until they fell asleep with exhaustion.

When he was awake, and dressed, Paolo called the lawyer he knew and arranged to meet him for lunch. Then he called his pianist friend with the house in Praiano. Yes. The house was free. The friend said he would telephone the woman from the village and ask her to go up and turn the heating on, prepare the beds, etc. He would also ask her to get in touch with the piano tuner in Salerno, and get him to come as soon as possible.

While Paolo was making these calls Maggie was still in bed. When she got up, and went to the bathroom, Paolo looked in her handbag and took her keys. He smiled as he did so; he was adopting Ralph's tactics.

He called to Maggie in the bathroom, "I'm going home to

change my clothes. I'll be back in about an hour. Are you going out?"

"No." She opened the bathroom door, and pointed toward Ralph's room. "I'll talk to him," she whispered.

Ralph was still in bed, Paolo presumed.

He walked home. He was sure that Ralph would agree to his plans. He was also sure that Maggie wouldn't want to come down to Praiano immediately with him, but would spend a few days with Ralph, alone, before joining him. He hoped so, in any case. If she did want to travel down with him, it would complicate matters slightly. Ralph's death would have to be put off for a week or ten days, until an excuse could be found for sending her up to Rome for a day and a night. Because it was essential that Ralph should die when he, Paolo, was—theoretically at least—in Praiano, and Maggie in the train, on her way down.

Again and again he congratulated himself on the beauty of his plan. Of course, it was a bore to have to go through all the motions of moving to Praiano for a month, and it was a bore to have lunch with the lawyer today, and make preparations for a wedding that wasn't going to take place. Nevertheless, it was essential that these steps be taken. He couldn't be careless, or lazy. Not in the execution of a masterpiece.

He stopped at the locksmith's on the way home and got copies of the keys to Maggie's apartment and street door.

When he was home he took a shower. As he stood under the hot water, feeling his body as he rubbed soap on it, feeling his hair and scalp as he rubbed shampoo into them, he realized that he was glad that Ralph had started following him; glad that the brother and sister had made *their* ludicrous marriage plans for him. He was glad to be doing what he was doing. He *wanted* to kill Ralph.

He would be great. Greater. That object which he had made, that object which was his body and mind, which functioned so well, and of which he was always in control, would now function even more perfectly.

He had said to Maggie that Christopher could have been great; and he had meant it. But Christopher had wanted an excuse, a justification, for greatness—hadn't found greatness, in itself, satisfaction enough. He had thought that if he made an object of himself, it was necessary to do something with that object. Give it away to someone. To Maggie, for example. That had been his mistake. He had come near to greatness, as if approaching the summit of a mountain. But he had trembled before its height, and had descended to the plains; to a world created by the judgment and definition of others; to a flat, safe world. Only having seen the mountain, and the view from its peak, he couldn't, quite, forget it, and had made a last desperate effort to scale it. But in his panic he had taken the most difficult route, and had fallen to his death.

Paolo wondered whether he should telephone a few people he knew, and tell them he was going away for two months. But there was no point; he wasn't. As soon as Ralph was dead he would come back to Rome.

When he was out of the shower, and dressed, he looked through his telephone book at the names and numbers of everyone he knew—all those casual, pleasant acquaintances—and thought that it would be nice when, next week, he could start seeing them all again; talking with them, eating with them, laughing with them, and going to bed with some of them. Next week . . . Only Elaine would have to be dropped. She had been too close to him; she had seen the last days of his old self. He wondered if all those other people, when he saw them again, would notice that he was different. That he was greater.

He smiled to himself.

At twelve he went back to Maggie's. She opened the door to him. She looked bright and happy. Her shoulders seemed less hunched than usual, her bosom larger. She kissed him on the mouth.

"We don't have to leave immediately," Paolo said. "I feel like a drink." In fact, as usual now, he was feeling excited, and wanted to make love. But there wasn't time for that.

As Maggie poured him a whiskey he slipped her keys back into her handbag. Then he said, "Well? Have you spoken to Ralph?"

Maggie smiled. "Yes. He thinks it's a good idea. But really—when do you want to go?"

"It depends how long it takes to get everything fixed—and on how much Alfredo can do for us. But hopefully, the day after to-morrow. It's best to leave very early in the morning. Otherwise it can take all day. You have to get the train to Naples, change stations and take another little train down to Sorrento, and then take a bus along the coast to Praiano. The journey's a bore. But if you catch the first train for Naples in the morning—it leaves at five o'clock, as I remember—there are fairly good connections. That way you get to Praiano at about eleven."

"Well, I must stay for a few more days. Just to make sure Ralph's okay. And that he really means it when he says he wants me to go."

"Fine. And when you do come I'll meet you at the bus stop, and have lunch cooking. The house is a mile or so up the hill above the village."

They had lunch with Alfredo, the lawyer, who told them what they had to do, and where they had to go, to make their arrangements for their marriage.

They started that afternoon, and were at it all the next day, and the day after. But by five o'clock on that third day, they had finished. They had been to the American embassy and signed and sworn to documents, to the prefecture, and to the Births, Marriages, and Deaths office. They had stood in endless lines, filled in innumerable forms, and answered absurd questions. But Paolo had stood up to the ordeal better than Maggie; it seemed to depress her—almost, Paolo feared, made her feel that her joke had gone too far. He encouraged her, and tried to cheer her up; for himself, most of the time, his permanent excitement made all the waiting and the bureaucracy, if not fun, at least bearable.

As they walked to Via Francesco Crispi, when it was all over, Maggie said, "So you'll leave tomorrow morning?"

"Yes. Five o'clock."

"Will you stay with me tonight?"

"No, I don't think so." He smiled at her. "I'll have to get up at four. If I stay with you I'm not going to get any sleep at all. But I'll come up with you now, for an hour or two. Have a coffee, or something." He squeezed her arm.

He had said coffee euphemistically, but in fact he did only have a coffee, because when they went into the apartment, Ralph was waiting for them.

It was the first time Paolo had been with the brother and sister together, and he felt awkward. He sat in the living room with Ralph while Maggie made the coffee, and neither of them spoke.

When Maggie returned, Ralph said, "So you're leaving?"

"Tomorrow morning."

"And you?" the boy said to his sister.

"I think probably Thursday or Friday."

Ralph nodded. "Good," he murmured. "I'm glad."

Paolo wondered whether he should make an effort to be friendly, but decided not to. It would be unnatural; and he must be natural at all costs. He mustn't arouse any suspicions.

They sat and drank their coffee in silence.

When they had finished Paolo said to Maggie, "Well, I guess I'll go now."

"Come with me a moment," the girl said.

She led Paolo to her bedroom and closed the door. "Ralph *would* be here now." She made a face, smiled, put her arms around Paolo, and kissed him.

"Do you have a pen?"

"Yes."

"I'll give you the telephone number in Praiano so you can call me to confirm when you're coming."

"Okay. And you call me if—you change your mind."

"I can't, can I?" Paolo said with a wry smile. He kissed Maggie on the forehead. "I'll see you soon."

As they went back into the living room, Ralph said, "Paolo, are you walking home?"

"Yes, I guess so."

"Good. I'll come with you. I want to talk to you."

Paolo glanced at Maggie, and the girl shrugged her shoulders. Paolo winked at her.

She stood at the door of the apartment and watched as they got into the elevator.

"See you soon," she said.

Ralph didn't speak in the elevator. But when he was in the street, hopping along beside Paolo, he said cheerfully, "So that's all settled."

"You happy?"

"Yes, very."

"Will you be all right here on your own?"

"Oh, sure." He slipped his arm through Paolo's. "You don't know how glad I'll be to be on my own."

Paolo was embarrassed with the boy on his arm, but he didn't think it mattered if it showed. He said, feeling like a solicitous elder brother, "Yes?"

"Yes. You know I've never ever been on my own. I lived with my father and then I went to live with Maggie and we went almost everywhere together and—well, Maggie's always treated me as if I were sick. I mean, not just this damned thing"—he tapped his bad leg—"but sick-sick-sick. And so I guess I've come to act as if I were sick. It did mean I didn't have to work in London. I wouldn't have minded particularly, and I did suggest it once, but Maggie wouldn't hear of it. She made enough money for us to live on, and we didn't have expensive tastes, and so if it made her happy that I didn't work, I didn't. I was quite happy myself. I stayed home and read and planned murders and went for walks, and I became Maggie's sick brother." He squeezed Paolo's arm. "You know, you and I have something in common, I'm afraid," he added with a grin. "You act as if you're great, and I act as if I'm sick."

Paolo smiled.

"I expect people to treat me as if I'm sick now. It'll be an experience being on my own. I might be forced to act well." He pursed his lips. "I doubt it, though. Most people are only too happy to act like I'm sick. Like Maggie does."

"But you love Maggie, don't you?" Paolo said, solicitously still.

"Of course I love Maggie. And Maggie loves me. Only I don't want her to end up hating me. And she might if we went on living together. She'd start to resent me. Think I was stopping her from leading a normal life. She'd never leave me, of course —unless I told her to—because she knows quite well that I only stop her from leading a normal life because she wants me to. But anyway—"

They walked along, arm in arm, and Paolo forgot to be embarrassed by his lame companion. He thought of what Elaine had said about Maggie, and wondered if not only Maggie was using him to get rid of Ralph, but also Ralph was using him to get rid of Maggie. Probably. At least in part. Only they had chosen the wrong person. They had chosen someone who wouldn't be used. Oh, Maggie would be free of Ralph, and Ralph would be free of Maggie—but Ralph would be dead. And then he wondered if, instead of choosing the wrong person, they had deeply, instinctively, chosen the right person. Someone who would be capable of going beyond their merely spoken wishes and interpreting their profoundest feelings. They had chosen someone as a composer chooses the ideal interpreter of his music. They had chosen someone great. Paolo Levin.

He walked along with the cripple on his arm, and felt almost proud of the boy; as if he were leading an obscene bride to a sacrificial pyre.

"But, Ralph," he said gently, "if you want to be alone, if you're glad that Maggie's going to come with me—marry me—why did you say you might kill yourself?"

Ralph hesitated before replying. Eventually he said, "Because I don't know if I shall be able to bear being well. I mean—I don't know if it'll be any different once the novelty has worn off. Maggie and everyone I ever meet treats me as if I were sick because they want to. I mean, people are like that. You are. But I guess I let them treat me as sick because I want to be treated that way. So if I want to—" He sighed. "Oh, I don't know. I don't really care. That's the trouble. I want to see Maggie happy, so she'll always love me. But there's nothing else in the world that interests me. I don't even like music like Maggie does. Oh, I like it. It passes the time. But anything that involves my body disgusts me, and anything that doesn't"—he laughed, briefly—"well, I've never come across anything that didn't. I guess you don't *believe*, as they say, and I guess I don't either. But my father did—he occasionally used to read the Bible. 'If thy right eye offend thee, pluck it out.' He would always leave it open on that page, for me to read probably. Maybe just so he wouldn't feel so bad about hating me, and leaving me in London. But anyway, I always used to think that my whole body offended me, so I should pluck the whole damned thing out." He laughed again. "But who knows. When Maggie leaves me I might suddenly develop all sorts of interests —start working or something. But I doubt it. When Christopher died and I found out you'd killed him, I realized that it was people like you who ruled the earth, and that sick people like me were necessary just to take all your mess on ourselves. And I'm not trying to be deep. It happens every day. If I go into a shop I can see the expression on the clerk's face. Pity and hatred. I know it's natural. But that doesn't matter so much. I could stand that. You know, I could think I was more intelligent or more *something* than that shopclerk. What matters is that though people pity me and hate me they *want* me to be like I am, so they can cast out their devils into me. And I'm fucked if I'm going to live sixty or seventy years on this planet just to give satisfaction to stupid ugly ignorant people."

Paolo glanced at the boy. There were tears in his eyes.

"But, like I said, the really twisted thing is that though all those people want me to be like I am, *I* like being like I am. I like to think I'm the soul of the so-called strong. I want them to despise me. It makes them stronger, and it makes me more necessary for them. So they depend on me. I show them up. You know that saying about if there wasn't a God it'd be necessary to invent one? Well, it's the same with me. If people like you—and even Maggie— didn't have people like me, you'd have to make us. Otherwise you couldn't stand yourselves." Again Ralph sighed. "But it's all so complicated and unimportant really. I just think that if you don't like living you should stop—and I don't know if I do."

"Ralph. This is sort of—" Paolo bowed his head. "But why did you fall in love with me?"

"Because I thought you were the strongest person I'd ever seen," the boy said quickly.

They didn't speak again until they reached Paolo's house.

"Are you coming up?" Paolo asked.

"No, I won't come up."

They looked at each other.

"I didn't really come with you to complain about being a cripple, I just wanted—" He looked around as if afraid of being overheard. Paolo moved with him through his street door until they stood at the foot of the stairs.

"I just wanted to ask you if—well, as you are going to marry Maggie, it does mean you killed Christopher, doesn't it?"

"No," Paolo said. He wanted to add, "I'm sorry." But there was nothing to be sorry for. He would have liked to tell the boy he had killed Christopher—as a sort of farewell present to him. He said, "I really didn't, Ralph."

Ralph looked into his eyes, and murmured, "Then I just came to say goodbye, and hope everything goes well in Praiano, and I'll see you on the twentieth of December if not before." He jerked forward and tried to kiss Paolo; but Paolo stepped back.

Ralph smiled, shrugged, and turned to hop away.

Next morning Paolo caught the train to Naples. By eleven-thirty he was in the house at Praiano, had unpacked, put his clothes away, and telephoned the woman in the village who looked after the house. He asked her if she could come up every day for the next few days at least, and clean for him.

She said yes and they agreed about money.

He went up onto the roof of the house, which was built in Arab style and set above the headland between Praiano and Posi-tano. Looking down at the sea, glittering in the sun, and at the beautiful coastline, he hoped the weather would stay fine for at least five days. He breathed in the clear clean air and thought that perhaps, when everything was over, he would stay down here till the 15th of December. It was so calm and peaceful, and though he felt very relaxed about what he was going to do, he might feel nervous after he had done it, and need somewhere quiet to stay. Of course, he would have to talk to the police, and answer ques-tions, and it might be difficult to find quiet even in Praiano.

The piano tuner came that afternoon, and after he had left Paolo went to bed and slept for three hours.

Maggie called him at eight to find out if he had arrived safely, and to tell him that she would be down on Thursday morning.

Paolo went down to the village, and had dinner in a restaurant.

Next morning he took the bus into Salerno, went to a car rental firm, and asked for a car for two weeks. He couldn't say for five days; it might sound suspicious later.

He drove slowly back to Praiano, along the winding cliff road. He hated driving, but he had taken his test seven years before and kept up his license in case of emergency. He was glad, now, that he had. Because this was an emergency. He parked the car in a parking lot below the village, almost empty now, at the end of the season. He wanted as few people as possible to know he had a car—or to know when he used it.

That afternoon the sun was so warm that he decided, in spite of the date, to take a swim. It took him twenty-five minutes to walk down from the house to the small rocky cove that was the nearest beach, and when he arrived he found that there were three other people lying there. They looked Scandinavian. Paolo greeted them; they started talking.

They stayed on the beach till five o'clock, then he invited the Swedes—two young men and a girl—up to his house for drinks and dinner.

They left at one in the morning and agreed to meet on the beach the following day, if the weather was fine.

It was.

And the day after.

Paolo said, "My wife's coming down to join me tomorrow, so I don't know if I'll be coming down here. Maybe later."

Long-haired, pretty, Ingrid said, "We're leaving tomorrow, anyway."

Bo—one of the young men—said, "We must have a last dinner tonight."

"No, I'm sorry, I can't," Paolo said quickly. "I have to get the house cleaned and ready."

The Swedes laughed. "Come on," they said. "We'll help you, afterward."

"No, I'm sorry," Paolo said again. He hoped he hadn't sounded rude. But it didn't really matter if he had. Tomorrow they would be gone. He wouldn't be able to use them as witnesses to prove he had spent the night in Praiano—he couldn't have done, anyway, because he wasn't going to—but neither would the police be able to use them as witnesses to prove that he hadn't. They would be on the road somewhere—or perhaps already back in Stockholm —by the time the police were called.

As Paolo walked up to the house he suddenly realized that it might be a long time before the police were called and Ralph was discovered. Because, in fact, there was absolutely no reason for him to be discovered immediately. He had been assuming that corpses couldn't lie around for days. But of course they could. Maggie would probably try to call Ralph from Praiano, and she might be worried when she didn't get any reply. But she would do no more than worry. She would think that he had gone off some-where. She wouldn't think of going up to Rome to see him—or at least not for a fortnight or so. And all that time he would be lying, dead, on his bed.

The idea was disturbing. Paolo saw that he might have to spend two months in Praiano whether he wanted to or not; although, he supposed, he could always find an excuse for Maggie and him to go up to Rome—to see the lawyer, maybe. And to find the stiff skeletal body of a crippled boy with a bullet in his brain.

When he reached the house he called Maggie to check that she was coming. She said she was packed and ready, and would see him tomorrow. She was going to bed early and setting the alarm for four, so she'd be in plenty of time for the train.

Paolo made himself a big dinner, ate, then went to bed and set his own alarm for eleven. He would have five hours of sleep.

At eleven he got up and dressed without turning any lights on. He dressed in a thick sweater and heavy jacket over his trousers, and slipped out of the house.

He walked down the hill, treading quietly. He didn't want anyone to see him. Luckily, by the time he got to the village there were very few people about, and he easily avoided them by slip-ping up side alleys, or into doorways.

He looked at his watch. Eleven-fifteen. Without hurrying he should be in Rome by four-fifteen at the latest. He would wait until just before five; Maggie would certainly have left for the station by then. He would go up to her apartment, let himself in, go to Ralph's room, pick up the gun from the bedside table, put it against the sleeping boy's head, and pull the trigger. Then he would wipe his own fingerprints off the gun, press Ralph's right hand around it—or if he could find a pair of the boy's gloves, put a glove on his right hand—and then place gun and hand in a suitable position. It would take only a few seconds.

He would drive back to Praiano, and should be there by nine-thirty. He would drive faster on the way back. He would leave the car in the parking lot, take off his thick sweater and jacket, and walk up to the house.

Then he would walk down again and meet Maggie as she got off the bus from Sorrento.

He hoped the car wouldn't break down, or get a flat tire; but he didn't see why it should. It was a big, reliable-looking Ford.

As he was crossing the road to go to the parking lot a car came along fast. He pretended to be looking down at his watch, so his face wouldn't be seen and, possibly, remembered. But the car suddenly stopped, and a girl's voice called, "Paolo!"

He looked up. It was Ingrid, the Swedish girl. In the car with her were Bo and the other young man.

"You could have come with us," the girl shouted.

Paolo stared at her—at her long blonde hair hanging out of the car window. He hated her. He said, "I left something in the car."

Bo said, "You come and have a drink with us now." He had a sing-song voice. Paolo hated him. He hated them all. "No," he said. "I must go to bed."

"Oh, come on," Bo and the other man shouted.

"Come on," Ingrid said commandingly.

"No, I'm sorry." Paolo stood by the roadside and braced his legs, as if preparing to resist them if they tried to carry him away by force. He made himself smile and say, "Have a good trip to-morrow."

Ingrid said something that sounded like "Mooo"; but the car

was driving off into the darkness. Paolo waved, and he saw the silhouette of a hand waving back.

He was trembling. He hoped the car crashed. He hoped they got very drunk and drove off the edge of the cliff. What would happen if they didn't leave tomorrow, and if Ralph's body was, somehow, discovered immediately? If anyone asked them they would say they had seen him going down to his car.

He told himself not to be stupid. Why should anyone ask them anything? And Ralph's body wouldn't be discovered immediately. He told himself to keep calm.

He was in Rome by four. He parked his car in a small street three blocks away from Via Francesco Crispi. He sat in the car and smoked, and looked at his watch constantly. The time passed very slowly.

It was one minute to five. Time to go. He was cold, in spite of his thick clothes. He got out of the car and locked it, and started walking, quickly.

He met no one. He opened the street door and went, quietly, up the stairs. He unlocked the door of the apartment. The lock was well oiled and didn't make a sound. The door swung open. He closed it behind him. Then he paused to accustom his eyes to the darkness. He stood for a minute in the hall, breathing deeply but silently. He slipped off his shoes and started to creep through the living room. He went into the corridor that led off it. The door of Ralph's bedroom was open.

He could see the dark curly head lying on the white pillow. It was turned away from him. He was glad. He wouldn't have to see that face again. He heard the boy breathing. He was asleep. The room smelled of sleep—and, very faintly, of garlic. He tiptoed to the bedside. The gun was there. He picked it up. He wasn't nervous. He didn't hesitate. He leaned over the bed and put the gun to the side of the sleeping, curly head. He pulled the trigger.

8

The gun clicked; but nothing more happened. Paolo flushed. He pulled the trigger again, and this time the gun didn't even click. He stared at it, in the darkness. He had to cock it, perhaps. But he didn't know how. He didn't know anything about guns. Besides, it was so dark in the room. Maggie had said that Ralph always kept the thing loaded and cocked. He started to sweat. He would have to go out of the room and go into the living room and turn on a light and see if he could do something. There must be something simple he had to do. He was trembling. It was impossible that his plan shouldn't work because of some technical hitch. It had to work. It was perfect. He felt faint. He had to keep calm. He would go to the living room. He turned; and gasped.

Standing in the doorway, staring at him, was Ralph.

Paolo jerked his head around and looked at the bed. The dark room swayed. Ralph was sleeping in the bed. Ralph was staring at him. He was going to faint.

Ralph, in the doorway, wearing a pair of striped pajamas, put a finger to his lips and whispered, "Sssh. You'll wake her."

Again Paolo turned to the bed. *Her.* It was Maggie lying there, sleeping in Ralph's bed. But Maggie was on the train, going down to Naples. . . .

He went toward Ralph. He had failed. He was ruined.

The boy stood still in the doorway, staring at him severely, like an awful, judging God. Paolo wanted to fall at his feet. He wanted to get out of that room. Ralph was blocking his way. He went up to the boy and stood in front of him. Their faces were inches apart. Ralph didn't lower his eyes. He continued to stare at Paolo. But very slowly he moved his head forward and kissed Paolo on the lips. Paolo closed his eyes.

He felt the soft wet lips. He opened his mouth. He felt the soft wet tongue entering it, exploring it. He was lost. He was being forgiven. He was saved. He pressed his face forward.

Finally Ralph withdrew his tongue and his lips. "Admit it now," he whispered. "Admit that you killed Christopher." Paolo opened his eyes. The boy was smiling slightly. "You can't deny it any more. But admit it. Tell me that you killed Christopher, or I'll wake Maggie and let her see you standing with that gun in your hand."

Paolo bowed his head. "Yes, Ralph," he whispered. "I killed Christopher."

Ralph took the gun from his hand and pushed past him. He replaced the gun on the bedside table. Then he returned to Paolo. "Come on."

Paolo stepped out into the corridor. Ralph followed him, and closed the bedroom door behind him. "Wait there," he whispered.

Paolo watched as the boy moved quietly down the corridor and went into the bathroom. He saw the light go on. Half a minute later Ralph came out wearing a pair of dark trousers, and pulling a sweater over his head.

They went together through the living room and into the hall. Paolo put his shoes on again. They left the apartment.

They didn't speak until they were in the elevator, when Ralph, still in a whisper, said, "I presume you have a car?"

Paolo nodded.

They went out into the street and walked to the car.

Ralph muttered, "Turn the heater on and drive around for a bit. I'm frozen."

Paolo started the engine and turned the heater on. The car pulled out.

"Well!" Ralph exclaimed, loudly and cheerfully. Paolo looked at him. The boy was grinning, and seemed delighted. "Well," he repeated. "I was right." He laughed. "Just as well."

"Why isn't Maggie going down to Naples?" Paolo's voice was small and hoarse. His throat was very dry.

"She couldn't, could she? It would have ruined my game."

"How did you know?"

"I didn't know. I just thought that possibly you weren't being sincere with me. So I thought—if he's not going to marry Maggie he must be planning something else. What? To kill me. How? I said to myself. The same way as he killed Christopher. When? I said to myself. The morning Maggie leaves. He'll drive up, do his dirty work, and then drive back. He'll be waiting for Maggie when she arrives. My body won't be discovered for a month, and by then everyone down where you're staying will be prepared to swear you were there the night I died—if anyone could tell after a month when I *had* died. It might have been in the day. Anytime. I didn't really think you'd do it. But I thought—just to be on the safe side. Not that I would have really minded for myself. But I had to know definitely if you had killed Christopher. I had to make sure that my great plans for you and Maggie weren't totally mad—that they were perfectly right and logical. And so I pretended to be very depressed yesterday and by ten o'clock last night managed to work myself up into a real state. I was crying. I told Maggie that I was losing her, that she was going away from me forever, that we had never been parted before and would never be together again." He giggled. "We talked and talked until one this morning, and I begged Maggie to stay with me for just one more day. We were lying on my bed talking. She was starting to fall asleep. She said you were expecting her. I said I'd call you. I was sure you wouldn't mind. I said she'd call. I told her to go to sleep. I said I *wanted* to speak to you. I called you at one-fifteen. There was no answer. Maggie went to sleep. I called you again at two. Still no answer. So I was sure I was right. When I called again at three and there was still no answer, I knew. So I unloaded the gun and left it there and waited. I thought you'd come at five, to give you time to drive back and be there to meet Maggie. I guessed you'd managed to get her keys off her sometime and get them copied." He smiled. "Stealing my tricks. And sure enough, at five, the door opens." He paused. "In fact, you made a mistake there—or at least were running a big risk. If Maggie had gone off at four-thirty to the station it was just possible I'd have gone to see her off—or at least been awake still at five, having said goodbye to her. But anyway"—he smiled patronizingly—"we'll let that pass."

"I didn't think," Paolo whispered. Then he said, "But how did you know I wouldn't bring my own gun?"

"Oh, people like you don't have guns. And anyway, you couldn't. You had to use my gun. I had to shoot myself with my own gun, didn't I? Maggie could have told the police if I hadn't. I guess there was a slight risk. You might have bought an identical gun. I thought of hiding in the wardrobe so I could watch you and be sure. But that would have been too melodramatic somehow. Me stepping out of the wardrobe saying, 'don't shoot.'" He giggled again.

"But however slight the risk, Maggie might have been killed."

"Yes," Ralph said thoughtfully. "She might."

They were driving down the Corso. Paolo glanced at the boy. "But how could you have risked that?" he insisted. "Even the smallest risk?"

"If you'd killed Maggie I'd really have had you, wouldn't I?" Ralph said quietly.

"But Maggie would have been dead."

"Yes. But she wouldn't have known anything about it. She wouldn't have suffered. She would have died happy. She was probably dreaming about you when you pulled the trigger. Sweet, isn't it?"

And they loved each other, Maggie and Ralph. He was right, Paolo thought, to have always distrusted and despised love.

"But don't draw any conclusions about what might have happened if you had killed Maggie. You're not in a position to do so. Besides, you don't understand anything." Ralph cleared his throat. "One thing I've always been meaning to ask you. Why did you put the glove on Christopher's hand? Why didn't you just wipe the gun clean—or wear gloves yourself—and then press his fingers on to it to make sure it looked like he'd shot himself?"

Could he deny it again now? Paolo wondered. Could he say, "I have no idea"? No. He had admitted it. He had to give Ralph an explanation.

"I couldn't bear to do that when he was dead. To touch his hand. To manipulate him. So I put the glove on. And besides, Christopher was the type who would have put a glove on to shoot himself. It would have seemed to him to make the act impersonal. There'd have been no actual contact between flesh and metal. It was in character."

Ralph nodded. "And how did you do it? Was Christopher asleep? What time was it?"

"About midday. No. He wasn't asleep. We were talking. He

was lying on his bed, and I was sitting on it. He had his eyes closed. I took the gun out of my pocket and stuck it against his head and pulled the trigger. He didn't open his eyes. He didn't see. He didn't know anything."

"And you thought he'd left you all his money?"

He had to satisfy the boy. "Yes," he said.

"Did he tell you that?"

"Yes."

"Then he probably closed his eyes because he knew you were going to kill him. He was like me. He knew what you were like. And he loved you. He knew you despised him for it. So he let you kill him. And he knew that that way he'd have you forever. As if by shooting him you'd made a child with him. A child you'd never be able to get rid of or disinherit." Ralph sounded as if he were talking to himself.

They were driving around the Colosseum. Paolo didn't know where else to go, what else to do, until he received fresh instructions.

Eventually he looked at Ralph. The boy had his eyes closed, and appeared to be sleeping.

"What shall I do?"

"You can take me home now. You've got a long drive ahead of you." Ralph opened his eyes and looked at his watch. "You should be back in Praiano by eleven at the latest. I'll get Maggie to call you then, to tell you that she'll be coming down tomorrow." He smiled. "I guess we should have the locks changed. Just in case you try again tomorrow morning. You could, couldn't you?"

Paolo didn't reply.

"But you won't. I could write a letter today to—oh, I don't know. A lawyer. Enclosing a note that should be opened in case of my death. Or something like that. Or I could tell Maggie."

"You won't, will you?"

"You won't, will you?" Ralph mimicked. "I don't see why I shouldn't. She should know exactly what she's marrying—if she doesn't already, which I suspect she might."

"Please don't tell her," Paolo pleaded. His voice sounded thin and childish. He remembered going to his brother's room, after he had pushed him off the roof and the little boy had been sent to bed. He remembered saying, "Please don't tell her."

"You don't want her to think you're a murderer?"

"No," Paolo whispered.

Ralph slipped down in his seat. "You know," he said, "you disgust me, Paolo. What do you *care* what people think of you? Why do you care if people think you're a murderer or anything else? You're supposed to be strong. Above all that." He laughed. "You know what your trouble is? You stick all those photographs on your wall and you've invented this great strong character called Paolo Levin—and it's only because you can't bear *this*." He jabbed a finger into Paolo's arm, and Paolo winced. "You're frightened of what people think of *this*"—again he jabbed—"frightened what people might say. That's why you can't bear people telling you they're in love with you. Because if they do they're in love with *this*"—yet again a jab—"and they're recognizing it, and making it exist, and *this*"—jab—"is a murderer. *This*"—jab—"is weak and despicable." He laughed. "Like me. But you're stupid. Because *this*"—and now he said it softly, and put his hand on Paolo's arm, and squeezed it—"is a musician. This is beautiful. What's on your wall is only a fake."

They didn't speak again until Paolo stopped the car outside the house in Via Francesco Crispi. Then, again, Ralph squeezed Paolo's arm and murmured, "The ridiculous thing is that the fake is what I'm in love with. Oh, well." He opened the door and slid his emaciated, crippled body out of the car. Then he stood on the sidewalk and waved as Paolo drove off, and called after him, "Have a good drive."

Paolo drove back to Praiano in a trance. He changed gear, braked, stopped for gas, and passed other cars without being conscious of what he was doing.

When he arrived, and had parked the car, he walked up to the house and lay down on his bed. He told himself that he was tired, and that he wanted to sleep. But he couldn't. He lay there for half an hour, then got up and went to his piano and started playing. He knew he was playing correctly, but he couldn't tell *how* he was playing. He was in a trance.

At twelve-thirty Maggie called. "I'm sorry," she said. "I

couldn't leave Ralph last night. He was so upset. What did he say when he phoned you?"

"Just that you were staying one more day. But he sounded upset. I guessed what it was. How is he today?"

"Oh, he seems quite cheerful today. He apologized for making a scene. I think he'll be all right now."

"So you'll come tomorrow?"

"Yes," Maggie said.

She would be there tomorrow. Quiet, self-effacing, implacable Maggie, who was going to be his wife.

That afternoon he drove the car back to Salerno, and returned it to the car rental firm. He said he had made a mistake; he wasn't going to be needing the car for two weeks after all.

Maggie arrived on the bus with three suitcases. She looked younger than Paolo had ever seen her, her mass of hair bright and floppy on her head; she even had some color in her cheeks. She was still dressed in black, but she wore a silver chain around her neck that relieved the gloom, and for the first time Paolo saw her as a girl, rather than as a problem to be solved, or as the mere female counterpart of Ralph. From now on, instead of being a thing to be dealt with, she was going to be a character to be lived with. She was going to be his wife.

"Hi," Paolo said. "How's Ralph?"

"He's fine now." She shook her head and obviously didn't want to talk about her brother. Why should she? Paolo thought. She had gotten rid of him. No wonder she looked happy.

"I've bought you a present," she said.

They walked slowly up to the house with the cases. When they arrived Maggie ran onto the roof and shouted down to Paolo, "It's beautiful here." She sounded like a little girl. It was impossible to believe he had made love with her, spent hours and days and nights with her. He had never seen her before. She ran down again and went into the house and started to unpack. Out of one of her cases she took a box. "That's for you."

It was a very expensive-looking Japanese camera.

"Thank you," Paolo said, and kissed her on the cheek. He felt

as if he were living in another century and had just met, for the
first time, the bride to whom he had already been married by
proxy. Theirs was an arranged marriage; yet they had arranged it
themselves. He was in a trance.

"I think it's a good one. They told me it's all automatic and
there are special lenses and everything. You must teach me how
to use it." She smiled happily. "I had an ulterior motive in buying
it, you see. I thought if you're going to be practicing all the time
I'll go out for walks and take photographs. It'll give me something to do. You will let me use it, won't you?" she said with mock
seriousness.

"I could hardly stop you," Paolo tried a smile. "We're more or
less a married couple, aren't we?"

"Don't sound so mournful." Maggie came over to him and
looked gravely into his eyes. "Do you think we could eat now?"
she said. "I'm starving."

Paolo wondered if she would get fat when she was older.

At twelve o'clock they walked down to the restaurant where
Paolo normally ate, and had lunch. Maggie paid the bill.

After lunch Paolo practiced. He stayed at the piano from two
till six. He wanted to stay in his trance forever. Maggie didn't talk
to him or interrupt him in any way. She stayed in the bedroom
most of the time; putting her clothes away, Paolo supposed,
or resting after her journey. When she did come into the living
room, she walked on tiptoe, and was obviously determined not
to disturb him; not to give him any reason to complain about the
girl he was going to marry.

He felt almost sorry for her and would have liked to stop, occasionally, and say something to her. But he didn't know what to
say, so he played and played, and as soon as he had finished one
piece he started another. Beethoven, Beethoven, and Beethoven.
For his last concert on December 15 he had to prepare the last
three sonatas.

But at six he was so tired he had to stop. He went into the
bedroom. Maggie was lying down, reading. He said, "I'm sorry
to be like this your first day here."

"No, I'm happy," the girl said. But Paolo could tell that she wasn't quite convinced. "Are you all right, Paolo?" she said. "You look terribly tired."

"I'm fine. What are you reading?"

"I'm rereading *Roderick Hudson*. Have you read it?"

"A long time ago."

"There's a lovely bit at the beginning. Where Cecilia says" —she read—" 'If Roman life doesn't do something substantial to make you happier, it increases tenfold your liability to moral misery.' " Maggie laid the book down and smiled. "Which does it do for you?"

"I honestly don't know," Paolo said. "Shall we go down to the village and do some shopping?"

"Do you want to go on playing? If you do, just tell me where all the shops are and I'll go by myself. I don't mind."

"No, I'll come with you."

"Are you sure?"

"Yes. I feel like a break."

He did feel like a break; but all the time he wandered from shop to shop with Maggie—he asked for what they wanted, and she paid—he wished he could be sitting, safely, at his piano.

Back home again, Maggie said, "Are you going to play some more?"

He was too tired. But he said, "I think I will. For a while."

"I'll go on with my book then. Or I might sleep for a couple of hours. I'm exhausted."

"I won't disturb you if I play?"

"Oh, no. Really."

That was what living together was going to be like.

At eight-thirty he stopped playing. Maggie was sleeping. She was in bed, and had pulled the covers over her, so that all that could be seen of her was her brown curly hair. Her face was turned away from the door. Paolo felt weak, and sick. He went over to the bed and sat on it. He could hear the girl breathing; breathing as deeply and regularly as she had the night before last, when he had held a gun against her head, and pulled the trigger.

Oh, it was all so mad. And he was so tired. He put his hand on the shape of Maggie's shoulder and shook it gently. "Come on," he said. "Wake up. It's time for dinner."

They prepared the meal together, and ate by candlelight. Afterward they turned on the television—a small portable set.

"Why don't we take it into the bedroom and watch it in bed?" Maggie said. "It'll be more comfortable."

Paolo nodded. "I think I'll take a bath first. I'm cold." He was cold, though the house was heated—and though the weather was still quite warm, and hardly called for heat.

By the time he had had his bath Maggie was sitting up in bed, wearing a white linen night dress. Paolo, naked, got in beside her. She leaned over and kissed him. He smiled vaguely at her, and then turned toward the television. He knew that she was puzzled and confused, but there was nothing he could do about it. She kissed his shoulder and said, "You smell good."

Paolo smiled at the television.

After a few minutes he put his arm around her and she rested her head on his chest.

He watched television and slowly fell asleep.

As soon as he woke—at eight—in the morning, he got up. He wanted to be dressed before Maggie woke.

He wondered how long it would be before they had to talk about their situation; or at least before he had to give some explanation about his lack of desire to make love. A day or two, he supposed. A week at the most. And it wasn't only that he had no desire; he knew that even had he had the desire, he would be incapable of doing anything. It wasn't going to be temporary, either; it was going to continue, and continue. He had a vision of a flat, dull landscape stretching away into the distance, populated by only Maggie and himself. A frustrated, hysterical Maggie, and an impotent, helpless Paolo. Trying to understand each other, trying to explain; then lying, and fighting, and picking at each other, and hating each other. . . .

When he was dressed he went into the kitchen and made some

coffee. He took it to Maggie in bed. She was awake. He wondered if she had been awake earlier, when he had gotten up.

He showed her how the camera worked. It was fairly simple.

Maggie said, "Well, the only thing to do is go out and try. Trial and error. I'll learn."

"Do you have film in it?"

"Yes. Black and white for the moment. Till I know what I'm doing. Then I'll get some color film."

She went out at ten, and stayed out till one.

Paolo practiced.

When Maggie returned she said, "If they do come out I should have some beautiful pictures. But it's a shame they're not in color. It's such a gorgeous day. And all the colors—" She smiled. "I've never seen anything so beautiful in my whole life. I love it here."

"More than Rome?"

"Yes. I was too nervous when I was in Rome. Never having been abroad before. But here—oh, I love it. I walked down to the beach. There's a path around the edge of the cliff and I walked all along it."

"It leads to a nightclub that's built into the cliff. The Africana."

"I saw it. That path must have cost a fortune. It's almost a mile long."

"It's a very expensive nightclub."

"Can we go there?" Maggie said eagerly.

"We can go anywhere," Paolo said. He heard that he sounded sour, though he didn't mean to be. "But the season's over."

Maggie looked hurt. "I think I'll take a bus into Positano this afternoon. Are you going to go on practicing?"

"Yes," Paolo said. Then, in an attempt to make up for his sourness, "I'm afraid so."

"Oh, no," Maggie sounded indignant. "I'm glad. How did it go this morning?"

"Well, I think."

They had lunch, and after Maggie had washed the dishes, she went out again with her camera. Paolo went to the piano.

Maggie returned at six; she had a bath. Paolo was still playing. He played till eight-thirty.

They made dinner together, ate, and then watched the television in the living room. They hardly spoke to each other.

At eleven Paolo said, "I'm tired. I'm going to bed."

"I'll stay and see the end of the program." It was a very boring documentary about life in provincial France. Maggie said, in an explanatory tone, "I'm sure this is the best way to learn Italian."

Paolo was still awake when Maggie came to bed, but she didn't turn on the light.

When she was lying beside him Paolo whispered, "I'm sorry, Maggie."

"I know." The girl was silent for a while, but then went on, "It's difficult for me, too. It's all suddenly stopped being a game, hasn't it? You said it was going to happen, and it has. It's all become real. And I've suddenly got cold feet. It's only now that it's become real that it's become really mad. At least for me. I guess for you it's worse. I mean—if I feel like this, at least I chose it. I planned it all with Ralph, didn't I? Only in a way I thought it was all a game. But now—and for you—" She sighed.

"Let's not talk about it," Paolo said. "We must pretend, as I said."

He *had* said it. But when he had said it he hadn't meant it. That had been part of his plan. But his plan had gone wrong, and Ralph was alive, and he was here, with Maggie, and he was going to have to pretend—to the end of his life, maybe, or to the end of Ralph's life.

He realized that the trance he was in was a state of misery. Yes. Perhaps that was what he would always feel, from now on. That was the condition of marriage, of the loss of self. Misery. He fell asleep.

Paolo lived in a trance, and played the piano for at least eight hours a day. Maggie kept the house clean, did the shopping, cooked, washed dishes, washed their clothes, went out for walks with her camera, read. They had no physical contact; in fact, they consciously avoided touching each other, even in the most casual way. They never bumped into each other. When they were eating they never reached for the salt at the same time. When, occasionally, Paolo accompanied Maggie down to the village to do the shopping, she would never hand him a bag to carry. She would leave it on the counter of the shop, and glance at him, dumbly, to pick it up.

Yet with every day that they grew further apart physically, they were, in spite of everything, getting to know each other; and Paolo couldn't help admitting to himself that he really did like Maggie. Before, in Rome, his physical excitement and desire to make love with her had been caused by the unnaturalness, the foreignness, of the situation; but now that the situation had become, even if grotesquely, normal, she was no longer an object in which, virtually, he liked to masturbate, with his brain full of confused fantasies, fears, and dreams. She was a human being; and while he wasn't able to cope with her in relation to himself, he became aware that, as a human being, she was one of the nicest he had ever met. She was never cheap or mean in her opinions, and she was never pretentious. She didn't, as Elaine had done, try to laugh away the world and its sorrows, nor view them with earnest satisfaction or despairing rejection. In a way, Paolo realized, she considered the world as she considered the affair she had created with him; as a game, but as a game to be played seriously. A game which had no rules, but which had a logic, albeit an apparently irrational one.

There was in fact only one thing about her that annoyed him occasionally, and that her naiveté, with regard to both herself and the world. But that was explained, he guessed, by the life she had led until recently, and would soon change.

She called Ralph a few times during their first two weeks in Praiano; he was well, he said, enjoying himself in Rome, and hoped they were happy. He told Maggie to give his love to Paolo.

Maggie's photographs turned out well; she had them developed at a shop in the village. At the beginning of the third week she bought a roll of color film, which she used in a day. She had to send it away to be developed. She bought another roll, and used that in a day, too. She said to Paolo, "I'm going to get some more black and white ones until these come back and I see how they are. When we go back to Rome I think I'll learn how to develop them myself. I think it would be nice."

So the next morning she again bought some black and white film. But that day—November 21—the weather, which had been glorious for so long, broke, and it started to rain, and the wind blew. Maggie was forced to stay indoors, and couldn't use the film.

She sat in the living room and listened to Paolo as he played. She read. She looked out of the creaking windows, down the rocky hill to the sea—gray and white and stormy.

The weather, or Maggie's continual presence, or the fact that he couldn't—or didn't let himself—get up from the piano for a moment, gave Paolo a headache. At five o'clock he told Maggie, crossly, that he was going to take some aspirin and go to bed. She said, "It's honestly not my fault."

Paolo made an effort. He swallowed. Then he bowed his head and said, "No, I'm sorry. I think I'm just terribly tired."

He went to bed, and slept through till six o'clock the next morning. When he woke he heard the rain falling on the flat roof of the house, and he had a feeling of gray, tired panic. For another day Maggie would stay indoors all the time.

But she didn't. She put on a black raincoat she had brought with her and told Paolo she was going to run down to the village to buy an umbrella.

She was out of the house until one-fifteen.

When she returned Paolo said, "Where've you been? You must be soaked."

"Only my feet. I'll go and put them in hot water. It's marvelous out. Wild."

"Maggie," Paolo said. His voice sounded false to him. "This can't go on."

She stared at him, then turned away before replying. "It won't," she said. "Don't worry. The weather'll clear in a couple of days." She went, quickly, into the bathroom. She had chosen to misunderstand him.

He sighed.

As they were eating their lunch Paolo said, "Listen, Maggie. This weather's going to go on for at least a while now. You can't go out all the time. You'll catch pneumonia or something."

Maggie put her fork down and looked at the table. "What do you want me to do?" She sounded resigned, hopeless.

"I don't know."

They sat in silence. Paolo felt sick.

"Does it really worry you so much if I'm around the house reading? I could stay in the bedroom if you don't want me in here." She was near to tears.

Paolo looked up at her. "It's not that you worry me. It's just thinking of you sitting here—I feel I should talk to you, say something to you. Keep you company." He told himself that he was being sincere; he hoped he sounded it.

Maggie sat still. Silent and miserable. Perhaps she would say, "All right, I'll go. The game's over. I'm sorry." But she didn't. She sat there, and said nothing, and it occurred to Paolo that even if she wanted to leave him she wouldn't be able to. Ralph wouldn't let her. She was as much of a prisoner as he was.

"Listen," he said. "Would you like me to call Ralph and ask him to come down? Just for a few days. A week. He'll be company for you. Would you like that?"

Maggie looked up finally. She seemed surprised. "Yes, I'd like that," she said slowly. "But what about you?"

"I don't mind. If you two were together I wouldn't worry about you being bored. You could—oh, I don't know. Play cards. Talk. Go for walks."

"Thanks a lot," Maggie snapped. She was blushing, and angry. But then she frowned and said, "Would you like me to ask Ralph to come?"

"Yes," Paolo said. "But only for your sake."

Maggie stood abruptly up and let her napkin fall to the floor. Without picking it up, she went to the telephone and dialed a number.

"Ralph," she said. "Paolo would like you to come and stay with us for a week. Would you like to come?"

Ralph was coming the next morning. Paolo felt agitated that

afternoon; agitated as he had been that first week, when Ralph had started following him. Only now there was a difference: his agitation didn't prevent him from playing. He played all afternoon, accurately and well. He was still in a trance, but he was coming around. He felt as if he were waking from a deep sleep. Vague intimations of consciousness were starting to seep into his brain; a dim awareness that there was going to be another day.

He realized that Maggie had spoken the truth on the telephone. He did want Ralph to come.

That night, for the first time since Maggie had arrived in Praiano, they made love.

9

In the morning it was still raining. Maggie said, "I'm glad Ralph's coming."

Paolo got up and dressed and went to the piano; Maggie walked down to the village to shop.

As she was leaving the house Paolo said, "Why don't you buy a bottle of Champagne if they have one. We'll have a celebration lunch."

"Okay," Maggie said. She looked puzzled.

When she returned she went into the kitchen to prepare the food. She stayed there until it was time for the bus from Sorrento to arrive. "I'll go down to meet Ralph," she said.

Paolo stopped playing. "I'll come with you. He might have some cases to carry."

"We can manage. You keep on playing."

"No, really, I'll come and help."

"Okay," Maggie said.

Ralph had one suitcase. He kissed his sister, smiled, said hello to Paolo and gave him, without saying anything more, the case.

They walked slowly up to the house. It had stopped raining, and Ralph looked around him and said, "It's beautiful here."

He sounded happy but not, as Maggie had done when she had arrived, impressed.

"You should have seen it last week when it was sunny," Maggie said. "Then it was really beautiful."

They had a long lunch. They all talked and laughed; Ralph told them what he had been doing on his own in Rome. Then he told Paolo—aided by Maggie—more about his Bible-reading, businessman father. Paolo told them about his parents, and about his aunt Mary; he didn't mention that he had seen them recently. They talked about music. Paolo—aided by Maggie—told Ralph about Elaine. They talked, and ate, and drank, and laughed, and Maggie showed Ralph the photographs she had taken. Paolo said, "Maggie bought the camera for me but I haven't been allowed to use it yet."

"Do you like it?" Ralph said shyly. "I helped to choose it."

"Yes, I like it very much."

Still shyly, Ralph said, "I've got presents for both of you in my case. But nothing big. Just little things."

A white silk head scarf for Maggie; a red sweater for Paolo.

At four Paolo returned to the piano. Though it had started to rain again, Maggie said, "I'll take Ralph for a walk."

They were gone till six-thirty. They came back with wet feet and red faces. A red face didn't suit Ralph; it made him look feverish, like an overexcited skeleton.

Paolo heard Maggie whisper, "We mustn't disturb Paolo." He would, in fact, have liked to be disturbed, but he kept playing, and Maggie and Ralph went into the bedroom; he heard them talking.

He practiced till eight, and then they all helped to prepare dinner.

After dinner they played cards until midnight; then they made up Ralph's bed—a collapsible bed that was usually kept in a cupboard in the living room—and wished the boy good night.

Paolo and Maggie made love; but only when they heard, by the sound of his breathing, that Ralph was asleep.

Next morning Paolo got up early and went down to the village and bought some brioches, then returned to the house and made coffee and took it to Ralph and Maggie in their respective beds. Maggie said, "Oh, thank you," but Ralph said nothing. He smiled secretively at Paolo, as if he were an emperor receiving no more than was due to him from his favorite.

Paolo went to the piano and started playing; Ralph lay in his striped pajamas and listened. Maggie was still in bed.

After an hour or so Ralph said, "Will you play something for me?"

"What do you want to hear?"

"What you played in Milan that day. Schubert's posthumous sonata."

Paolo bowed his head. "It lasts forty minutes," he murmured.

"Yes, I know. I'd like to hear it."

Paolo breathed in deeply. "All right," he said obediently.

He started to play. Forty minutes. It was nothing. An hour. Two hours. Ten hours. What did it matter? He would play for as long as Ralph told him to play. He could do anything. Play. Kill. Get married. Live. Die.

Nothing was impossible.

He heard Maggie come out of the bedroom and sit behind him. When he reached the end of the first movement the girl said, "I have to go down to the village. Are you coming, Ralph?"

"No."

"Okay. I won't be long."

Paolo glanced at her, and she gave him a smile that seemed, to him, to be full of tenderness and compassion. Suddenly he wanted to get up and put his head on her bosom and his arms around her and lie on the bed with her and rest. But he couldn't. He had to play for Ralph.

He started the second movement.

By the time Maggie returned he had almost finished. When he struck the last note she said, "Thank you."

Ralph, behind him, clapped his hands and cried, "*Bravo, maestro!*"

Paolo closed his eyes for a second, then turned to the grinning crippled boy. "Anything else?"

"No, I want you to help me clean," Maggie said quickly. She sounded angry, and frightened.

At lunch, whenever Maggie wasn't looking, Ralph caught Paolo's eye and winked or grinned at him. Maggie never saw, but she knew, or felt, that something was going on, and she didn't speak or try to make conversation. The meal was as uncomfortable and tense as the one the day before had been pleasant and relaxed.

When they had finished eating Maggie said, "Ralph, come and help me wash the dishes."

"I'll help too," Paolo said.

"No. You get on with your practicing," the girl almost snapped at him.

As they were washing up Paolo heard her say, "Ralph, when we're finished, let's go out for a walk and leave Paolo in peace."

He heard Ralph say petulantly, "No, I want to stay and listen to Paolo."

Paolo played louder, so as not to hear them; but Maggie, as if she were a singer being accompanied, raised her voice.

"*Please.*" And then, "I'm not going alone and we can't stay and worry Paolo."

"But it's raining."

"It isn't at the moment, and even if it is, we can wrap up. *Please*, Ralph." Her voice rose higher.

Then Paolo heard no more until Maggie came out of the kitchen, walked across the living room, went into the bedroom, and slammed the door. He stopped playing and turned around. A minute later Maggie came out of the bedroom wearing her black raincoat and carrying another, beige one—Ralph had hung his clothes in the only wardrobe in the house, in the bedroom—and went back to the kitchen, where Ralph was standing, waiting for her. She handed him the beige coat and said to Paolo, "We're going out for a walk."

Paolo nodded. "It's stopped raining, I think. For the moment, anyway."

"It won't hurt us if it starts again."

"Can we take the camera?" Ralph said sulkily.

"Yes, if you like," Maggie replied without looking at him. "But come along."

She ran back into the bedroom, picked up the camera, went across to Ralph, took his arm, repeated quietly, "Come along," and led him to the front door. "See you later," she said to Paolo, pushed Ralph forward, and followed him, closing the door behind her.

Paolo looked at his hands. They were shaking. He wanted to cry. He swallowed, and blinked. He had tears in his eyes. He put his hands on the keyboard and told them to start playing. Anything. He struck a chord. Then another. What could it be the start of? Anything. Something by Chopin. Yes. That would do. Anything would do. He couldn't let Maggie and Ralph destroy him.

At seven-thirty the telephone rang. It was Maggie. She said that she and Ralph had taken the bus into Positano. They were going to stay there for dinner. Maybe they would go to a movie. She didn't know. She told Paolo not to wait up for them. It wasn't a request. It was an order.

He was in bed when they returned, but he wasn't asleep. Maggie undressed and got into bed beside him, and lay still and tense on her back.

They lay side by side until they heard that Ralph was asleep, and then Paolo stretched out a hand and touched Maggie's thigh. He wanted to make love. Or perhaps he didn't want to, but had to, as if he had an irritation in the blood. But Maggie took his hand and pushed it away. He replaced it. She pushed it away again. She whispered, "Oh, why did you want him to come?" Then she turned her back to him, and Paolo lay still, looking up into the darkness. How long had they taken to destroy and damn him? Just two months. It seemed impossible. Or was it Christopher's fault? He cursed all three of them. Then he cursed Elaine and his parents, his aunt and his brother and Natasha and Jean—everyone he knew or had ever known. Finally, he cursed himself.

Next morning he woke early but lay in bed until he heard Ralph call, "Paolo, are you awake?"

He looked at Maggie's back, and wondered if she was still asleep.

"Yes," he called back.

Maggie turned over and muttered, "Uh?"

"Nothing," he whispered to her.

"Will you make me some coffee?" Ralph called.

Maggie opened her eyes sleepily and watched Paolo as he got out of bed. "Where are you going?"

"To make some coffee."

Maggie closed her eyes again and said softly, "Oh, God."

Paolo made the coffee and gave a cup to Ralph, then went into the bedroom to give one to Maggie. But she was out of bed, with her skirt on, pulling her black sweater over her head. He put the cup on the bedside table. She looked at it but didn't thank him for it.

Paolo sat down on the edge of the bed. Maggie finished dressing. "You can have the coffee if you like," she said. "I don't feel like any."

"Why not?"

"I just don't feel like it." She was putting her raincoat on.

"Where are you going?"

"Out."

"Where to?"

"For a walk." She grabbed the camera from the top of the chest of drawers and left the room. He heard her say to Ralph, "Get up when you've had your coffee and fold the bedclothes up and put the bed in the corner. And don't take too long. It makes the whole room look squalid. Oh, and open the window when you're dressed. It smells in here."

Ralph didn't ask her where she was going.

Paolo heard the front door closing. He went into the living room and looked sheepishly at Ralph. Ralph grinned. "Poor Maggie. She wishes she hadn't asked me to come."

"I suggested it."

"I know."

"What did you do yesterday afternoon?"

"Went for a walk. Maggie tried to persuade me to go back to Rome. I said no. She said she had a feeling something terrible was going to happen if I stayed. I told her I was staying. So she suggested we go to Positano. We looked at some not very interesting churches, had dinner, saw half an Italian Western, and caught the last bus back. You?"

"I practiced till eight. Then I went down to the restaurant in the village. Then I came back and went to bed."

"What are you going to do today?"

"Practice. And you?"

"Depends on Maggie. But I'd like to stay in. I'll get sick if I keep on getting wet." He paused. "Could you turn the bath on for me? I want a bath. Then I'll clear up in here."

While Ralph was in his bath Paolo folded up his bedclothes, pushed the collapsible bed into a corner of the room, opened a window, then sat down at the piano.

When Ralph came out of the bathroom he said to Paolo's back, "That's very kind of you," and laughed.

Maggie returned at a quarter to one; neither Ralph nor Paolo asked where she had been.

She said, "Ralph, will you come and help me prepare lunch?"

"No, I don't feel like it."

She went, on her own, to prepare lunch.

After lunch she said, "Will you at least help me with the dishes?"

"No," said Ralph.

"I'll help you," Paolo said.

"Fuck the dishes. They can stay dirty." She got up from the table and put her raincoat on again. "And I suppose," she said to her brother, "that if I ask you to come out with me you'll say no?"

"You suppose right."

Maggie made dinner. When they had eaten she said, "Well, there are no more clean plates now, so either we don't eat, someone washes them up, or we go down to the restaurant."

"It's easier if we go down to the restaurant, isn't it?" Ralph said.

Maggie shrugged. Paolo said, "I'll go down tomorrow and ask Signora Drusiani if she'll come and clean up. I might as well ask her to come every day, if she can."

"Do what you like," Maggie said.

They watched the television after dinner; Paolo made up Ralph's bed for him at eleven o'clock.

When he was in bed himself he again wanted to make love with Maggie, but he didn't touch her because he knew she wouldn't let him.

After he had made Ralph's coffee next morning he went down into Praiano. He hadn't seen Signora Drusiani since the day before Maggie had been due to arrive. Now he told her that though his wife had come, she had brought her brother with her, and the housework and the cooking were proving too much for her. He asked her if she would come up every morning to clean, and prepare lunch for them.

The tiny, gray-haired woman in her black dress smiled slightly scornfully and said she would be up in half an hour.

As Paolo walked back to the house he met Maggie. "You going for a walk?" he said.

"Yes."

"I've seen Signora Drusiani. She'll come up every day and clean and make lunch for us."

"Good," Maggie said without enthusiasm.

Paolo smiled. "I told you you'd get used to having someone come and look after you. You'll be wearing your fur coat soon."

Maggie didn't smile. She gazed at him for a while, with her shoulders hunched, and her big pale hands hanging limply by her side. Then she said, "Oh, Paolo—" She looked as if she was about to burst into tears. She started to walk away, and called, without looking around, "Ralph's waiting for you up at the house."

Paolo went on up.

He played, Ralph listened; Signora Drusiani cleaned and then started to cook.

At one Maggie returned, and the three of them ate in silence.

Three more days passed. The weather didn't improve; it got worse, if anything. It not only rained much of the time, but the wind, which had been warm, became cold.

On the morning of the seventh day of Ralph's stay, Paolo was in the kitchen making coffee when he heard, in the living room, Maggie say to her brother, "Ralph, you've been here a week now. I think you should go back to Rome."

Paolo stopped what he was doing and waited for Ralph's reply.

He heard the boy whine, "I don't want to, Maggie."

He heard Maggie say, "I'm sorry, my love, but you've got to. This whole situation is impossible."

He heard Ralph say, slowly and firmly, "Maggie, I'm not going back to Rome. I don't want to go back. I don't want to be on my own there. I like it here. I like being here with you and Paolo. I want to stay and I'm going to stay. There." Then the tone of the voice changed; the boy sounded sly, and amused, as he added, "Ask Paolo what he thinks."

Paolo turned toward the door of the kitchen with a coffee cup in his hand. Maggie stood in front of him and stared at him challengingly. Her mouth was open, her jaw twisted to one side, and her white cheeks had red spots on them. "Well?" she said.

Paolo smiled weakly and shrugged his shoulders. He didn't know what to say. He looked at Maggie, and thought how strange it was that only a few months ago this girl had been a secretary in an office in London. Her principal preoccupations had been how to pay the rent, what to do in the evening, and how many letters she had to type. Now she ruled the world. She must have been an efficient secretary; quiet and conscientious and cheerful, if a little bit closed. He couldn't imagine her gossiping with any of the other girls in the office, or even volunteering information about herself to her employer. She would have been liked, he imagined, but would have been held slightly in awe; people would have said, "She's a foreigner, of course," and dismissed her like that. She had been nothing; now she was great.

She turned away and closed the kitchen door behind her. He heard her walking about. He heard Ralph saying, "Where are you going?"

Maggie didn't reply.

The front door opened.

Ralph called, "Maggie, where are you going?"

He heard the boy run out of the living room.

He opened the kitchen door. The front door was open, and there was no sign of either brother or sister. He put the coffee cup down and went to the piano and started playing. It was the only thing in the world he could do.

Some time later Ralph returned, smiling. He went up to Paolo and put his hand on his neck. "Maggie's gone out to take some photographs."

Paolo stopped playing and turned. "What are you going to do, Ralph?" he said.

"I'm going to stay, of course."

"For how long?"

"Forever, sort of."

Paolo stood up and started to walk around the room. What happened now? What did he do? What did any of them do?

He glanced through the open door of the bedroom. Maggie's black raincoat was lying on the bed. He jerked around to Ralph. "Maggie's gone out without her coat. She'll catch her death of cold."

Ralph sat down and looked at his fingers. "Would you like that?" he said.

"What do you mean?"

"I mean, would you like it if Maggie died?"

Paolo looked again at the black raincoat. "Where's Maggie gone?" he whispered.

"I told you." Ralph grinned secretively at his fingers. "She's gone out to take some photographs, like she does every morning."

"But—"

"What would you do if Maggie killed herself? Would you be happy?"

Paolo stared at the boy.

Ralph stood up. He said huskily, "If Maggie killed herself you'd be stuck with me. You know that, don't you? Just like if you'd shot her." He walked toward Paolo.

Paolo didn't move.

Ralph whispered, "Or would you like that anyway? Would you like me to tell Maggie when she comes back that *she* has to go away, go back to Rome? Shall I tell her that you and I are going to stay here together?" He was very close. "Is that what you'd really like? It would be fairer in a way, wouldn't it? After all, it was me who wanted to come to Italy for you. And it was me who fell in love with you. If Maggie went back to Rome she'd find someone else easily enough. She's pretty, she's rich, she's not stupid. It's not that she'd be left alone, like I will be if you marry her. Shall we tell Maggie to go, Paolo? Do you want me to stay with you? You do, don't you? You just don't want to admit it. Tell me. Go on."

Paolo took a step back. He had to get away. It didn't matter where to. He just had to get out of this house.

Ralph shot out a hand and grabbed his arm. "Don't run away. Where would you go to, in any case?"

Paolo froze.

"Come on," the boy said. "Let's go and find Maggie. Let's go and tell her to go away."

Paolo tried to take another step, but Ralph was holding him tightly.

Then, suddenly, the boy relaxed. He laughed and said, "I'll tell you what. We'll have a *race*." He paused, and appeared to be thinking. Then he went on. "We'll have a race from here to that nightclub in the cliff. And if I win we tell Maggie to go away. And if you win—well, you marry Maggie. I'll go away." He laughed again. "You lose either way, don't you? But this way it'll be up to chance. And you can let me win if you want to. Don't you think that's fair? After all, I'm almost giving you a free choice. And you are *so* strong, aren't you?" He released Paolo's arm, and his thin hand tapped Paolo's chest. "You're marvelous physically, aren't you?" He went down on his knees and put his hands around Paolo's thighs. "Just *feel* that strength!" He giggled. His hands slipped down to Paolo's calves. "Such athlete's legs!"

Then he stood up and looked Paolo in the face. He was no longer smiling. He narrowed his eyes and whispered, urgently, "You better run if you want to save your life, because I'm going to race you down that hill to that club and I'm going to win. I swear it. And you needn't look so fucking confident because I'm going to run as if all the forces of hell were behind me."

Paolo took a step back. He had to run. He had to get away.

Then he heard someone coming up to the front door. A

woman, singing. Signora Drusiani. He was saved. He moved over to the piano stool and sat down. The woman came in the front door. She said, *"Buon giorno"* cheerfully to Paolo, and smiled at Ralph.

Paolo said, *"Buon giorno, signora."* He put his hands on the keyboard.

Ralph said, *"Noi facciamo—"* he stopped. "Paolo, how do you say 'a race'?"

Paolo turned. He saw Ralph looking at Signora Drusiani, and he saw the woman waiting, smilingly, for what Ralph had to say.

"Corsa," Paolo murmured.

"Oh, yes. Signora Drusiani. *Noi facciamo una corsa. Chi—* Paolo, how do you say who do you think will win?"

"Chi vincerà, secondo Lei?" Paolo said to the woman.

"Come, una corsa?"

"Sì, una corsa. Io e Ralph. Facciamo una corsa fin'alla spiaggia."

The woman looked at them both, and laughed. *"Mi prende in giro, Signor Paolo."* She pointed at Ralph's leg and said, *"Con quella gamba!"*

"What did she say?"

"That we're making fun of her. Because of your leg."

Ralph smiled happily. *"Io molto forte,"* he said. Then, to Paolo, "Tell her to start us."

Paolo winked at the small woman, as if to tell her that it was all a joke, and that she should humor Ralph.

"Ci da la 'via," he said.

Signora Drusiani raised her arm in her black dress as if she had a gun in her hand. *"Pronti?"* she said with a smile.

"You ready?" Paolo asked Ralph.

Ralph nodded. Paolo stood up. He said, *"Sì,"* to Signora Drusiani.

"Allora. Uno, due, tre—via!"

Paolo reached the front door first, opened it, and ran out, calling *"Arrivederci"* over his shoulder to Signora Drusiani. He heard her call back a long, cheerful *"Arrivederci"*; she was obviously amused by the antics of the crazy foreigners—and probably slightly moved, thinking that Paolo was playing this game with Ralph to make the boy feel normal and healthy.

He heard Ralph call, "*Ciao.*"

"*Ciao, ciao,*" Signora Drusiani called.

It was very cold out. Paolo ran down the steps by the side of the house, and along the lane leading to the little road that wound down the hill. He heard Ralph's syncopated steps behind him.

The quickest way was to take the little road down the hill for about half a mile, then go onto the main coast road for another half mile, then, just before it reached the village proper, take the fork that led down to the beach. Then across the sand, up the steps carved into the cliff, along the path, and so to the night-club.

Paolo ran, and, though the wind was cold on his face, he started to sweat. He could still hear Ralph behind him, though more faintly now. He glanced over his shoulder. The boy was about a hundred yards behind, lurching along, his good leg pounding up and down, his bad leg swinging madly, but obviously doing some work.

There were a few people on the road, and they stopped and stared at the odd spectacle coming toward them. As Paolo passed them he slowed down slightly, and smiled, to assure them that this race *was* just a game. He glanced over his shoulder and saw that Ralph did the same, the scarlet thin face under its mop of hair beaming at astonished men and women.

At one moment a young boy on a bicycle came down the hill; he rode along beside Paolo and asked him why he was running. Paolo told him he was having a race. "*Con quello?*" the boy said contemptuously, pointing over his shoulder toward Ralph. "*Sì, sì,*" Paolo said. The boy rode on down the hill, and waved, and Paolo waved back, and smiled.

He wondered why he smiled. He wondered why he was making this pretense that the race was just a game, that he was enjoying himself. It was, he supposed, because he was ashamed of himself, disgusted with himself, and frightened, and he didn't want anyone to see it. He didn't want anyone to think that he, Paolo Levin, was running away, was running for his life.

He ran on down the winding road, and didn't look back again until he reached the main road. He thought that if Ralph was far enough behind him he would stop for a moment, to get his breath. But Ralph wasn't far enough behind; in fact, he had closed the distance between them slightly.

Paolo ran on, sweating. He ran as fast as he could along the flat road. He looked over his shoulder. Ralph was gaining on him. That wild, uncoordinated skeleton was running faster than he. It was impossible. He ran on, ran as fast as he could. He had a pain in his chest and stomach. He looked over his shoulder more and more frequently; every time Ralph was nearer. He was only fifty yards away now. Maybe less. He thought of what the boy had said. "You can let me win if you want to." But he didn't want to. He wanted to get away from him. He was running as fast as he could. Maybe it had something to do with the wind. There was a gale blowing in his face. It was slowing him down. Ralph was so much thinner that it probably affected him less.

Paolo ran on. He looked over his shoulder. He was holding his own now. Yes, a good fifty yards. He passed an old man, and forced himself to smile. It was starting to rain, and great clouds were racing toward him in the gray sky. He ran on. He looked over his shoulder. Sixty yards.

He reached the fork down to the beach. He wouldn't meet anyone coming along there. He could forget about having to keep a smile ready. He was in agony. His legs. His chest. His shoulders. His stomach. He wouldn't look back until he reached the beach. But when he did Ralph was only forty yards behind. He ran down some steps and jumped onto the pebbles. He still had to go all that way along the cliff path.

He ran across the beach. He looked around. He tripped.

He went sprawling onto the pebbles, but was picking himself up even as he fell. His ankle was twisted. He couldn't run. He had to run. His knee hurt, and his hand was cut. There was blood on it. His ankle screamed at him to stop. He couldn't stop. He had to run.

He reached the steps to the cliff path and lurched up them. He couldn't go on. He was almost hopping. He was the same as Ralph. Two cripples racing for their lives. But Ralph knew how to run with only one good leg, and he didn't. It was fair now. They were the same. He ran, lurched, hopped on, around a bend, out of sight of the beach. Thirty feet below him the sea was crashing against the rocks, and he couldn't tell if it was sweat on his face, or tears, or rain, or spray. He ran on. He looked over his shoulder. Ralph was only twenty yards behind now. He was smiling; scarlet and smiling. There were another eight hundred yards or so to run.

He ran on. Fifty yards. A hundred yards. The path hadn't yet rounded the headland. Above there was the cliff, below him there was the stormy sea, behind him there was Ralph, and ahead of him— He fell again, and this time he knew he wouldn't be able to get up. Ralph was going to win. It was impossible. Paolo was on his hands and knees. His hands, with blood on them, were resting on some stones and shale that must have fallen down the cliff. He grasped one of the stones in his right hand, and as he heard Ralph about to run past him he managed to throw the stone, under his left arm, at the boy. Incredibly, it hit him, in the stomach. Ralph stopped and gasped, winded. Paolo turned his whole body on the path, so he was kneeling, facing the boy. He looked at his hand. There was strength in it. It was a pianist's hand. But it had been mere luck that his stone had hit its target. He looked up at Ralph. He took another stone in his hand. The boy took a step back, his thin body heaving.

Paolo realized that he was heaving, too. He was sobbing with exhaustion. Very slowly, with the stone in his hand, he stood up. Ralph took another step back, and pressed himself up against the cliff. Paolo, as if he were playing ball with a small child, lobbed the stone at him. It hit him on the throat, and the thin hands fluttered at the boy's side, as if they were going to rise to protect his body. But then they lay still. Ralph whispered, "Please don't, Paolo."

Paolo didn't take his eyes off him for a second as he stooped down and picked up two more stones. Big ones. He lobbed again. The first hit Ralph's shoulder and the second his stomach again. Ralph made a terrible choking noise. He opened his mouth, then closed it. He was leaning back, thin and crippled, against the cliff. Paolo stooped and picked up two more stones. Then he stood and faced the boy. They stared at each other, and were both very still, and the world became silent, in spite of the sea crashing below them, and the howling gale. Then once more Ralph opened his mouth, and a thin high-pitched scream came out. "Don't," he screamed. "Please, Paolo. Don't."

Paolo lobbed. The stone hit Ralph on the forehead. He fell. Paolo waited. Eventually Ralph managed to get to his feet again. There was blood on his forehead, in his eye, on his nose, and in his mouth. He was no longer looking at Paolo. Perhaps he could no longer see. Paolo lobbed again. The stone caught Ralph on the cheek. He didn't fall. Blood started to trickle down his cheek, to join at his chin with the other little dark red stream that was coming from his forehead. Then he started to whimper, like a small, beaten animal. "No. Please don't," he said. But now he was talking to himself, in a little childish voice. "Please don't, Paolo. Please don't. Please don't."

Paolo stooped and picked up a handful of smaller stones. This time he hurled them at the boy. Ralph staggered sideways, broken, limp, like a rag doll, and leaned against the waist-high green railings on the sea side of the path. He was making tiny staccato sounds—gasps, cries, whimpers. He raised his head and opened his eyes very wide, as if searching for some help in the sky.

Paolo stooped and picked up another handful of stones. He raised his arm; but he didn't throw. He saw that he had done enough. Ralph was dying.

Then, suddenly, the boy seemed to find the help he had been searching for. A smile came to his wide, bloody lips, and he raised an arm. He made a strange little movement with his rag-doll body, a strange little flick of his back, a strange little leap. And then he was falling slowly, backward, over the green rail. Falling down the cliff into the stormy, crashing sea.

Paolo heard a cry in the wind; and he realized why the boy had smiled and raised an arm. He turned, and looked up the cliff at the help Ralph had been searching for, and found. There, with her camera in her hands, and wearing a white fur coat, was Maggie.

Paolo looked up at the girl, and she looked down at him. He couldn't see the expression on her face. He couldn't tell, even, how far away she was. His eyes weren't focusing, and great blobs of darkness were floating up from inside him. He tried to call out to her; but as he opened his mouth he felt himself fainting, and falling onto the path.

When he came to Maggie was leaning over the rails, staring down at the sea. He lay still for a while, and tried to catch his breath. Then he got slowly, agonizingly, to his feet, and leaned on the rail beside her. Looking down he saw Ralph's body. It was on the crest of an enormous wave, and seemed to be flying through the air. It smashed down onto the rocks. It was dragged back into the sea. It rose on another wave. It smashed down again. Maggie's hands were gripping the rail. She rested her head on them. Paolo saw that she was crying.

He whispered, "He killed himself. He threw himself over."

Maggie didn't appear to have heard him. He could hear her crying now, her sobs getting louder and louder.

Paolo looked down at his bloody hands. At his pianist's hands —his murderer's hands. The cut wasn't deep. He put his mouth on it and sucked it. It had almost stopped bleeding. He stood on the path and waited for Maggie to say something, or do something. Great Maggie, the ruler of the earth.

He waited for five minutes, and still Maggie stood there, with her forehead resting on her knuckles. He could no longer hear her crying, and her body was no longer shaking. But then he realized that she was waiting for him. He looked at her, bent over, in her white fur that was wet and bedraggled. He looked at the brown leather strap of the camera around her neck. What had she taken photographs of? Him, stoning her brother to death? Or just of Ralph leaning against the rail, with blood streaming down his face, smiling at her and waving? Or just of the stormy sea, and the sky? How much had she seen? How much did she know? He looked at her, and knew that he couldn't ask her; he could never ask her. Because whether she had photographed Ralph or not, she had seen him die. She had seen the blood on his face. Why hadn't she cried out earlier? Did she see him only at that last moment? Or had she known that it would have been useless to cry out—that Ralph would have died anyway? Or, loving him, had she wanted him to die?

He said, "Maggie, we must go and get the police."

She lifted her head and nodded. Her eyes were red and her nose was running. She started to walk down the path toward the beach. Paolo followed her. His ankle hurt still, but it wasn't badly sprained. He was cold, and soaked, a fine steady rain was falling, sweeping in huge gray veils across the sea.

He took her arm. She didn't snatch it away from him.

They walked together, unspeaking, down the steps, across the pebbled beach, up the road. Maggie started crying again. They walked up to the main road, and along into Praiano. People in the street, shopping under their umbrellas, stared at them.

They went to the *carabinieri*. Paolo said that Maggie's brother had fallen off the cliff path into the sea. Maggie stood by his side as he spoke; she didn't say a word.

Then things were taken out of their control, and became easier. Telephone calls were made. They were rushed to the beach in a car by the *carabinieri*. They led the men along the path; they showed the point where Ralph had fallen. Paolo leaned over and looked down. The broken body was wedged between two rocks.

"Is he still there?" Maggie whispered.

Paolo nodded.

They were taken back to the *carabinieri* station and given brandies. Someone found a dry sweater for Paolo. Maggie was asked if she wanted to take her wet coat off and put something else on. She didn't say a word; just shook her head violently, and clutched the coat to her, as if afraid that someone was going to pull it off her by force.

They were asked some formal questions—names, addresses,

nationalities—which Paolo answered for both himself and Maggie. Then a middle-aged officer asked how the tragedy had happened. Paolo told him that he and Ralph had decided as a sort of joke to have a race down to the beach from their house. He explained that Ralph was a cripple, but liked to live and act as normally as possible. He said that they had reached the cliff path when Ralph shouted out that he was too exhausted to run any more.

How far was he ahead of Ralph?

About twenty yards.

Wasn't that strange, if Ralph was a cripple?

Paolo said that he hadn't been running full out, of course, otherwise there'd have been no fun in it; he would have arrived half an hour before Ralph. Besides, he had twisted his ankle slightly, which had made the race fairer. In fact, he had been intending to let Ralph win. But anyway, Ralph had shouted out that he was too tired, and pulled himself up and sat on the railings with his back to the sea. And then, as Paolo was walking toward him, he suddenly toppled over backward. It looked almost as if he'd done it deliberately, or had fainted. Perhaps, Paolo suggested, that was the explanation. The boy had been so exhausted that he had passed out. It had been obvious, immediately, that nothing could be done for him. For one thing, Ralph must have died when he hit the rocks. For another, he was being smashed by the waves. And for another, there was no way down from the path to the water. Even if the boy hadn't died instantaneously, they couldn't have reached him or helped him.

"*E la signorina?*" the officer asked Paolo. But Maggie, finally, started to speak. She spoke, very slowly, in English, and paused at the end of every sentence so that Paolo could translate what she was saying.

"I was up the cliff taking photographs of the sky and the sea. I knew a place farther along the path where it was easy to climb up the cliff. I went there this morning at about nine because I saw that it was going to rain and I wanted some photographs of the rain coming in from the sea. I had told my brother that I was going down there, and he told me that he and Paolo would come down later to join me. I was waiting for them. I was up above the point where Ralph fell. From there I had a view of both sides of the headland—Praiano, Positano, the whole gulf. I had just taken a photograph of the sky. There was a shaft of sunlight through the clouds. Then I heard someone shout. I looked down and saw my brother leaning on the railings. When he saw me he smiled at me and waved and then—seemed to throw himself backward."

The officer asked Maggie, Paolo translating still, "He *threw* himself?"

"Yes."

"You don't think he fainted?"

"No. I'm sure he threw himself."

"You think he deliberately killed himself?"

"Yes, I think so."

"Had he any reason to kill himself?"

"I don't know. Possibly."

"What—?"

"Paolo and I are getting married next month. I've always looked after Ralph. We've been very close. I think he might have been jealous. Or if not jealous—I think he was afraid he would be a tie on me when I was married. He was afraid that I'd feel a greater obligation to him than to Paolo. He was afraid he might come between us. Then he was afraid I might resent him for this. He was afraid of being left alone. I don't know."

"Had he ever spoken about this?"

"Yes. Not in the last week, while he's been down here. But before, in Rome. Especially my last night there. I was supposed to come down one day at the beginning of this month, but Ralph was so upset I had to put off coming for a day."

"But this last week he's been happy?"

"Yes, very happy."

"How long was he going to stay down here for?"

"Today was the last day. He was leaving tomorrow."

"Was he unhappy about that?"

"He didn't say so. I think he was."

"And so you think he killed himself because he thought he might unwillingly come between you and your fiancé?"

"Yes, I think he killed himself to ensure that Paolo and I could have a happy, normal marriage."

Then Paolo was asked if Ralph had said anything to him about being unhappy; he said no, but he had sensed that the boy was disturbed.

And so the questioning went on.

Finally it was over, and a car took Maggie and Paolo up the hill to their house. Paolo was asked if he would come down to the station again later that day, when the body had been recovered from the sea. He said he would. Maggie was told it wouldn't be necessary for her to come down again that day. Tomorrow, or the day after, both of them would have to come, and proper statements would have to be drawn up, and signed.

They walked up the steps to the house in silence.

When they were inside Paolo went into the bathroom and turned on the hot water in the tub. He said to Maggie, "You'd better have a bath to warm you up. I'll have one after you."

Maggie whispered, "Yes."

Maggie was in bed when Paolo had had his bath. He got in beside her and touched her hand. She turned slowly toward him, and started crying. He held her sobbing body and stroked her thick, curly hair. Then he started crying too.

They clung to each other in the bed, crying for themselves, and for Ralph.

They were still clinging to each other two hours later when Paolo heard a knock at the door. He kissed Maggie on the forehead and gently extracted himself from her arms. He got up and pulled on a pair of jeans and a sweater and went to see who was there.

Signora Drusiani. Paolo saw from her expression that she had heard the news. He supposed that the whole village had heard the news by now; all the people he had smiled at as he had run down the hill, with Ralph pursuing him. Would they go to the police and say they had seen the fatal race? Would Signora Drusiani say that she had started them? What would she say? That they had been friendly as they left the house? Would she say they had been having a game? Probably. . . .

The little woman whispered that she had heard the news and

was so sorry, and wondered if she could do anything.

Paolo asked her if she would stay with Maggie while he went into Praiano and saw the carabinieri about Ralph's body.

Ralph had been hideously broken on the rocks. There were awful gashes all over his body and face, most of which was missing.

When Paolo returned to the house around seven, Signora Drusiani was sitting on the bed with Maggie's head in her lap. The girl's eyes were open, but she wasn't looking at anything. Signora Drusiani was stroking her hair with a little, arthritic hand.

Maggie didn't say a word all that evening and, as far as Paolo could tell, didn't sleep at all that night. He did, but only for a few minutes at a time.

Next morning Paolo said, "We must call your father, mustn't we?"

"Yes. I guess so."

They went down into the village and sent him a long telegram. Maggie said she didn't feel capable of speaking to him on the phone.

Her father called that evening. Paolo answered the phone. He told him that Ralph had fallen off a cliff.

The father said, "Who are you?" He had a voice like his daughter's; quiet, and apologetic.

"I'm a friend of Maggie's. Her fiancé. We're getting married soon."

"Maggie didn't tell me. I haven't heard from her for five months. Are you on holiday in Italy?"

"No. I live here."

"How is Maggie?"

"All right. I mean—as well as can be expected."

"When is the funeral?"

"I don't know. In a couple of days, I guess."

"Does Maggie want me to come over for it?" The man paused. "I wasn't very close to Ralph." He sounded even more apologetic.

Paolo put his hand over the receiver and whispered to Maggie, "Do you want him to come?"

"No."

"She says she can deal with everything."

"Can I speak to Maggie?"

Paolo pointed at the telephone and raised his eyebrows. Maggie nodded. She got up off the sofa and took the receiver and said, "Hello, Dad." She told him in a flat voice how Ralph had died. "No, there's no point ... Oh, yes, don't worry ... I came here on vacation and met him ... He's a pianist ... He'd come to stay with us for a week. I wanted him to meet Paolo ... No, he's American ... Oh Dad, I'm sorry." She started crying. "Yes. We'll try and come over sometime in the new year. Or you come here ... No, I'm quite sure. There'd be no point. Paolo's doing everything ... No, really, it'd just make me more miserable. I'd start crying as soon as I saw you. Please don't. Come in a few months, when I'm married, and happier. There's no point now. Please."

When she had finished speaking she said to Paolo, "Is there something in the kitchen? I must eat something."

For the next three days they spoke only formally together, mainly about the arrangements for Ralph's funeral.

Signora Drusiani was with them most of the time in the house. Paolo was glad of her presence, and was sure that Maggie was too. They both spoke to her more than they spoke to each other; to her they even managed to talk about the weather, and about her family, and about what was going on in the world.

Ralph's body was buried in Praiano. Maggie, Paolo, and Signora Drusiani were the only people present at the simple ceremony.

When it was over Signora Drusiani shook her head sorrowfully and said softly to Paolo, "*Ah, quella corsa.*"

Maggie heard her, and later, when she and Paolo were alone in the house, packing their bags, she said, "Was it true about the race?"

"Yes," Paolo said. And then, since they had finally started

talking about what had happened, he asked, "And was it true that you told Ralph where you'd be and he said we'd come down and join you?"

"Yes. He said to keep a watch out for you both."

"I was going to let him win," Paolo said.

They finished packing their bags in silence; but Paolo thought of all they had told the *carabinieri* and realized that they had, in fact, told the truth—the essential truth—about Ralph's death.

They went to Paolo's apartment when they returned to Rome; Maggie said, "I just don't feel up to seeing that other place yet."

But the next day she said, "You must practice. I'm going out for a walk. I might go over to the apartment." She took her camera with her.

Paolo started practicing. He played the three Beethoven sonatas he had to give at his concert, one after another, without a mistake. He rested for half an hour, and smoked a cigarette, then returned to the piano and played Schubert's posthumous sonata. As he played it he thought of Ralph; and he realized he was playing it for Ralph. Every note he struck, every chord, conjured Ralph. Ralph following him. Ralph kneeling by his bed. Ralph watching him as he shot Maggie with the unloaded gun. Ralph laughing. Ralph talking. Ralph angry. Ralph happy. Ralph in Rome. Ralph in Praiano; Ralph running after him, pursuing him, and leading him to Maggie. Ralph cowering against the cliff. Ralph screaming. Ralph being stoned to death. Ralph leaning against the railings. Ralph smiling, and waving. Ralph making that last great effort, and flinging himself backward. Ralph ensuring that his sister would get married to the man he—and possibly she—loved. Clever Ralph. Terrible, hideous, crippled Ralph. Making them all guilty. Saving them. Beautiful Ralph.

As he played, with these images of Ralph before him, he knew that he had never played so well in his life before; in fact, he felt that he had never played in his life before. He no longer felt he had to impose himself on the music; he no longer had to master it. He no longer felt frightened that, if he didn't master it, he would be lost and helpless in it. He stretched out his hands and played, and the music came to him; like a language he could finally understand. It came to him in Ralph's image, speaking of life, and death, and love—above all of love—and Paolo stretched out his hands, and welcomed it.

Maggie came in late that afternoon. She smiled slightly at Paolo. "I went over and cleaned up Ralph's room," she said. "It wasn't as terrible as I thought it would be. I threw his gun and his knives away. I fired the gun into the air first so it couldn't hurt anyone. But it wasn't loaded."

"I guess you're going to give that apartment up now?" Paolo said. He didn't look at Maggie as he spoke.

"I don't know," Maggie said quietly. "I mean—you're quite free now, Paolo. You know that, don't you? You don't have to marry me if you don't want to. You don't have to do anything you don't want to."

Paolo looked around the room. He wondered if she had brought her camera back with her. And if she had, was there film in it? The same film? Or had she stopped by a photographic shop and asked for the roll to be developed?

"I guess we can both live here until we find somewhere bigger," he said.

Maggie turned away from him. "I think I should keep mine for a little while," she said. "Just in case. And anyway, I've got quite a lot of junk there. I don't want to get in your way."

"You won't."

"But also I'd like someplace to mess around in on my own. I went to the English bookshop today and bought a book telling how to develop your own films. I thought I might use Ralph's room there as a darkroom." She sat down heavily in an armchair, and Paolo saw that she was blushing. She looked at her hands. "I've got to have some hobby to occupy my time while you're practicing, haven't I?" Then she said very quickly, "Please, Paolo, tell me whether you want me to stay or not?"

Paolo stared at her. He thought of her in Ralph's room, developing her photographs, and again he wondered how much she had been able to see from her vantage point up the cliff. He went over to the sofa and sat down. It didn't really matter. He could have easily, anytime in the last five days, destroyed that film. Maggie hadn't made any effort to hide her camera. He could so easily have opened it and exposed the film. But it hadn't even occurred to him to do so. He had known what images, what evidence, it might contain, and he hadn't destroyed it. And so—

He got up from the sofa and knelt on the floor in front of Maggie. He took her pale hands in his, and kissed them.

They went out to a restaurant and had an early dinner; by ten o'clock they were in bed. They made love, and fell asleep in each other's arms.

Next day Paolo practiced, and Maggie was out most of the time.

When she got in she said with a guilty smile, "I spent a whole lot of money today buying developing equipment and stuff."

Two days later when she came in in the afternoon she was carrying a packet. She said, "Look, Paolo." She tried to sound casual, but was obviously near to tears. She laid the packet on the table. Paolo left the piano and went to the table and sat down. He knew what would be in the packet.

The first photograph was of the house in Praiano. The second of the sea, taken from the beach. The third, too. The fourth was of Ralph standing, smiling at the camera.

"That was the last day he came out for a walk with me," Maggie murmured.

The fifth was of the sea—a stormy sea. Paolo guessed it had been taken from Maggie's lookout place on the cliff.

The sixth was of the stormy sea.

The seventh was of the sky, with sun shafts breaking through the wild clouds, and a mist of rain moving in off the water.

The eighth was of the stormy sea and sky.

The ninth was a photograph of Ralph leaning against the rails of the cliff path, with one arm raised in a wave. It was obviously Ralph, but the top right-hand corner of the photograph, where the face should have been, was smudged and blurred.

Maggie, behind Paolo, whispered, "I did something wrong there. Perhaps a drop of rain landed on the lens. Or perhaps I put my thumb there, or used too much developing fluid."

Paolo closed his eyes for a moment. "And the rest of them?"

"They didn't come out. I must have forgotten to wind the film on or something."

Paolo rested his head on the table. He wondered if Maggie was telling the truth. Probably not. But it was something he never wished to know—something he would never need to know as long as he, in his freedom, chose to stay with her. And he *was* free; Maggie herself had said so. He heard her leave the room and start doing something in the kitchen.

"Would you like some coffee?" she called.

Paolo, with his head on the table, said, "Maggie."

He heard her come back into the room.

"What would you have done if I'd told you the other day that I didn't want to marry you?"

He heard her come over to the table. He heard her gathering up the photographs and putting them back in the packet. She said, "I don't know. But—I was sure you wouldn't." He felt her hand on his head. "I was sure Ralph was right. He loved me too much to do anything wrong. He knew just what he was doing. Always. You thought he was terrible. But he was right." She paused. "He was, wasn't he?"

Paolo didn't move his head. "Yes," he said, "I guess he was. You know—that day. He said we had to have a race or else he would tell you to go away. He would have stayed with me. Would you have gone if he'd told you to?"

"Yes. But he must have known you'd race him."

"Did he know I'd lose?"

"Ralph knew *everything*," she said sadly, but fiercely. "He even knew how much we'd be able to bear." Then she lowered her voice to a whisper. "I think he even knew how terrible *we* were. Only I don't believe he would have called it terrible. He loved us. That's why he did so much for us. And that's why we had to do what he wanted." She cleared her throat, and gently squeezed the back of Paolo's neck. "Do you want some coffee?"

"Please," Paolo said.

He was nervous before his concert, more nervous than he had ever been before. His parents were in the audience; he had telephoned them and asked them to come—to meet Maggie, he had said.

Before he started playing he closed his eyes for a second and once again pictured Ralph's bloody, smiling face. He silently dedicated his performance to the boy; just as he knew he would dedicate every performance throughout his life to him. Then his nervousness left him, and he felt like a man returning to his family, and to the beloved country of his birth.

He told his parents he was going to marry Maggie, but he didn't tell them when, so they returned to Stresa after the concert. He did tell them, however, to write to his grandmother and tell her that within a month or so her grandson would be married.

"So you see," he said to Maggie, "I'm not marrying you for your money."

She laughed, and said, "No, but if you didn't marry me you wouldn't get any, would you?"

The day after the concert there was a review in one of the papers that made him—and Maggie—smile. "Paolo Levin," it read, "is a monster of technical virtuosity. So much so that at times he makes one forget the great, almost terrible humanity of these last Beethoven sonatas."

"What rubbish critics talk," Paolo said.

"Yes," Maggie smiled. "You never made me nervous for a second last night. You were wonderful." With her mouth twisting ironically sideways she added, "I fell in love with you last night."

They got married at the Campidoglio; the ceremony was very quick and painless. Paolo asked some people he knew casually to act as witnesses. He said to Maggie with a smile, "We can tell my friends later. There's no point in rubbing salt into the wounds."

They took a larger apartment, and Maggie gave up the apartment in Via Francesco Crispi; she said no more about having a darkroom, or pursuing her photographic hobby. In fact, Paolo never again saw the camera she had given him as a present.

He said to her one day, "You're happy to live in Italy, aren't you?"

Maggie shrugged. "Oh, sure," she said. "Countries are only a state of mind, in any case."

Later she said, "Besides, Ralph brought me to Italy. He knew I'd be happy here. He was always right."

Paolo liked living with her; they got on well together, his friends liked her—after a while even Elaine became friendly with her.

They had sex two or three times a week. "Is that average, above, or below?" Maggie asked.

"I don't know. But I guess average," Paolo said. "We're a pretty average couple."

Paolo practiced every day; not because he felt Maggie's presence obliged him to, but simply because to play the piano became a necessity to him. He remembered that he had thought that his playing had been a part of his life; now, he realized, it was his whole life; it was *him*.

Occasionally he would feel trapped by Maggie's presence, and would regret his unmarried days; but whenever he did Maggie sensed it, and announced that she was going away for a few days. Once she went to the States to visit her father; another time she returned to London.

While she was there she visited her former employer, and saw some people she had known, and returned to Italy with two concert dates in England for Paolo.

Pleased by her success as her husband's agent, she started to work at it, and soon was arranging dates, checking contracts, and getting recording work for him.

She worked harder as his reputation grew.

When she was away, or if she didn't accompany him to his concerts, Paolo would occasionally have casual sex with someone he met at a party or reception. Sometimes he enjoyed it, sometimes not. He never told Maggie, but he guessed she knew and didn't mind too much.

He did, however, after he had been separated from her for any length of time, tell her that he had missed her. She—and their relationship—became, in fact, as essential to him as the photographs on his bedroom wall had previously been. He supposed that, if she had asked him, he would have admitted that he loved her; but she never asked him, and though this irritated him some-times, and made him want to tell her without being asked, he thought it was probably for the best. She heard him playing, and he expressed himself through his music more honestly and com-pletely than he could ever have done with mere words.

There were no photographs in the bedroom of their new apartment, and only two in the whole place. They were small ones, kept in silver frames on a table in the living room, and were both of Ralph. One was Ralph standing, smiling at the camera; the picture taken on his last walk with Maggie. The other was Ralph leaning against the railings of the cliff path in Praiano, with his hand raised in a wave.

The face, which had been smudged in the photograph, Paolo, whenever he looked at it, added mentally. The bloody face, to which he had dedicated his life. The bloody face that smiled upward, as if in thanks to a world that called, or would call, Paolo Levin great.

Paolo Levin is an accomplished American concert pianist living in Rome. Intensely self-absorbed, Paolo values his independence above all else and has no desire to be trapped in the commitments of a relationship. But he can't seem to shake off the attentions of Ralph, the sinister crippled boy who is in love with Paolo and persists in stalking him.

One morning Paolo awakes in terror to find himself handcuffed to his bed with Ralph looming over him. Paolo's most precious parts – his hands – are to be forfeit unless he submits to Ralph's bizarre demands . . .

Described by one critic as "the master of modern horror," Hugh Fleetwood is the award-winning author of more than twenty volumes of fiction, including the classics *The Girl Who Passed for Normal* and *The Order of Death*. *Foreign Affairs* (1973), his third novel, is a wickedly compelling thriller whose unexpected twists and turns will keep readers on the edge of their seats until the shocking conclusion.

'I must repeat my admiration for the high promise shown in *Foreign Affairs*. Hugh Fleetwood appears much the most talented young English author I've come across in some time.'
– Peter Prince, *New Statesman*

'A gripping novel.' – *Books and Bookmen*

'A rich, gruesome, irresistibly readable book.' – *Sunday Times*

'Mr. Fleetwood can write like a dream . . . and really get into your head. He reaches down and stirs up with venomous delight the nameless, faceless things swimming far below the levels of consciousness.' – *Scotsman*

VALANCOURT BOOKS
www.valancourtbooks.com

ARCH OBOLER'S

house on fire

WITH A NEW INTRODUCTION BY
CHRISTOPHER CONLON

HOUSE ON FIRE

ARCH OBOLER was born in Chicago in 1907, the son of Jewish immigrants from Latvia. He grew up a voracious reader and early turned to writing, selling his first story when he was ten.

Recognizing radio as a powerful medium for storytelling, Oboler began writing radio scripts in his twenties, selling his first, *Futuristics*, to NBC in 1933. His big break came in 1936 when Wyllis Cooper departed the popular weekly radio horror program *Lights Out* and NBC invited Oboler to replace him. His first play, *Burial Services*, which ended in a young girl being buried alive, proved too much for audiences, and afterwards Oboler toned down the horror, relying largely on the strange and fantastic. But despite the show's extreme popularity, what Oboler really wanted to write about was Fascism, which he saw as more horrifying than any of the imaginary terrors on *Lights Out*.

During the 1930s, Oboler wrote and directed radio plays for other programs, often working with the premier stars of the day, such as Bob Hope, Gary Cooper, and Mae West. After Pearl Harbor, Oboler was able to realize his goal of writing anti-Fascist plays and created the new series *Plays for Americans*, weekly stories laced with wartime propaganda, starring James Stewart, Bette Davis, and others. He also revived *Lights Out*, working anti-Nazi messages into the weekly episodes.

Like Orson Welles, Oboler made the jump from radio to film; his directing credits include *Bewitched* (1945), a film noir about a murderer with a split personality that pre-dated *Psycho* by fifteen years; *Five* (1951), a post-apocalyptic science fiction film; and *Bwana Devil* (1952), the movie that sparked the 3D craze of the 1950s.

Oboler also wrote one drama for Broadway, *Night of the Auk* (1956), directed by Sidney Lumet with an all-star cast that featured Claude Rains, Christopher Plummer, and Dick York. Though it ran for only eight performances, one critic compared it favorably with another of that season's plays, Eugene O'Neill's *A Long Day's Journey into Night*; it was revived in New York in 2012. In 1969, his only novel, *House on Fire*, was published and earned comparisons to Ira Levin's *Rosemary's Baby*. Oboler died in California in 1987, aged 79.

CHRISTOPHER CONLON is a writer and editor best known for his Richard Matheson tribute anthology *He Is Legend*, which won the Bram Stoker Award and was a selection of the Science Fiction Book Club. His novels include the Stoker Award finalists *A Matrix of Angels* – "the most wrenching serial-killer novel of the past decade," according to *Booklist* – and *Midnight on Mourn Street*. Conlon lives in the Washington, D.C. area. Visit him online at christopherconlon.com.